訓練聽力　增加字彙

　　英語聽力是學習英語的重要一環，必須提早開始，長期訓練。而且要有計劃地反覆練習，絕不能只學聽單自認圖片，一定要聽句子，而且要逐漸拉長句子的內容，才能學習到英語的真諦。

　　本書分為〔上〕、〔中〕、〔下〕引導學生在學習上循序漸進，逐步加強，期望能在12年國教國中會考考試中，一舉拿下聽力的滿分。本書的另一特色為在快樂學習中增加單字的記憶和使用能力，透過反覆的聽力測驗，不但大量增加字彙的累積，在不知不覺中也學會了說與寫的能力，可謂一舉數得，而且輕鬆易得。

　　為減輕學生的聽力障礙，本書將考題敘述的每個句子及答案，都精心譯為中文，以供學生參考。

1. 隨時注意 7 個 W：who, when, what, where, which, why, how
也就是人、時、事、地、物、原因、狀態

2. 能夠與不能 (ability and inability)
常用字詞有：can, be able to, could, can't, couldn't, not be able to, neither

1)　　A: How many languages can you speak?
　　　B: I can/am able to speak three languages fluently.
　　翻譯：A：你能說幾種語言？
　　　　　B：我能流利的說三種語言。

2)　　A: Has he bought a new house?
　　　B: No. He's never been able to save money.
　　翻譯：A：他買新房子了嗎？
　　　　　B：不，他永遠沒有能力存錢。

3)　　A: I couldn't do the homework. It was too difficult.
　　　B: Neither could I.
　　翻譯：A：我不會做作業。太難了。
　　　　　B：我也不會。

3. 勸告與建議 (advice and suggestion)
常用字詞有：had better, I think, let's, OK, yes, good idea, sure, why not,

1) A: I've got a headache today.

　B: You'd better go to see the doctor./I think you should go to see the doctor.

　翻譯：A：我今天頭痛。

　　　　B：你最好去看醫生。我想你應該去看醫生。

2) A: I've got a terrible stomachache.

　B: You'd better not go on working.

　A: OK./All right./Thank you for your advice.

　翻譯：A：我的胃痛死了。

　　　　B：你最好不要上班。

　　　　C：好的/沒問題/謝謝你的勸告。

3) A: Let's go, shall we?

　B: Yes, let's./I'm afraid it's too early.

　翻譯：A：我們走吧，要不要？

　　　　B：好，走吧。/我怕太晚了。

4) A: What/How about going fishing now?

　B: That's a good idea./That sounds interesting./Sure. Why not?

　翻譯：A：現在去釣魚怎麼樣？

　　　　B：好主意。/聽起來很有趣。/當然，有何不可？

5) A: Let's go to the concert.

　B: I don't feel like it. Why don't we go to the beach instead?

　翻譯：A：我們去聽音樂會吧。

　　　　B：我不想去。我們為什麼不去海邊？

4. 同意與不同意 (agreement and disagreement)

常用字詞有：I think so. I hope so. I don't think so. I agree. I don't agree. So can I. Me too. Neither can I. I can't, either.

1) A: The book is interesting.

　B: I think so, too.

　翻譯：A：這本書很有趣。

　　　　B：我也這麼想。

2) A: Do you think people will be able to live on the moon in the future?

B: I hope so, but I don't think so.

翻譯：A：你認為人類將來能住到月球上嗎？

B：希望如此，但我不認為能夠。

3) A: This lesson is interesting, isn't it?

B: I don't think so./I'm afraid I can't agree with you./I'm afraid I don't quite agree with you./I'm afraid it isn't.

翻譯：A：這堂課很有趣，不是嗎？

B：我不這樣認為。恐怕我無法同意你。我恐怕不十分同意你。恐怕不是這樣。

4) A: I can swim well.

B: So can I./Me too.

翻譯：A：我很會游泳。

B：我也是。

5) A: I can't play the guitar.

B: Neither can I./I can't, either.

翻譯：A：我不會彈吉他。

B：我也不會。

5. 道歉 (Apology)

常用字詞有：Sorry. I'm sorry about ….

A: Sorry./I'm terribly sorry about that.

B: That's all right./Never mind./Don't worry.

翻譯：A：抱歉。關於那件事我非常抱歉。

B：沒關係。不要放在心上。不要擔心。

6. 讚賞 (Appreciation)

常用字詞有：That's a good idea. That sounds interesting. Fantastic! Amazing! Well done ! That's wonderful.

1) A: I've got the first prize.

B: Well done ! /You deserved to win./That's wonderful news.

翻譯：A：我得第一名。

B：真棒。你實至名歸。真是個棒消息。

2) A: We had a surprise birthday party on Saturday afternoon.

B: That was a super afternoon.

翻譯：A：星期六下午的生日聚會令人驚喜。

B：那是個超棒的下午。

3) A: He broke the world record for the two mile run.

B: Fantastic!/Amazing!

翻譯：A：他在兩英哩賽跑打破世界紀錄。

B：了不起。又驚又喜。

7. 肯定與不肯定 (certainty and uncertainty)

常用字詞有：sure, not sure, perhaps, maybe, possible, possibly,

1) A: Are you sure?

B: Yes, I am./No, I'm not.

翻譯：A：你確定嗎？

B：是的，我確定。不，我不確定。

2) A: When will Mary go to school?

B: Perhaps/Maybe she'll go at eight.

翻譯：A：Mary 何時上學？

B：或許 8 歲。

3) A: His ambition is to be an architect.

B: He'll possibly go to university after he leaves school.

翻譯：A：他的願望是當建築師。

B：他離開學校後可能要念大學。

8. 比較 (Comparison)

常用字詞有：as...as..., not so... as..., more... than..., less...than...,

1) A: How tall is Sue?

B: 1.6 meters. She's not so tall as Jane.

A: What about Mary?

B: She's as tall as Sue.

翻譯：A：Sue 身高多少。

B：160 公分。她不像 Jane 那麼高。

A：那 Mary 呢？

B：她跟 Sue 一樣高。

2) A: Which is more important, electricity or water?
B: It's hard to say.
翻譯：A：哪個比較重要，水還是電？
　　　　B：很難說。

9. 關心 (Concern)

常用字詞有：Is anything wrong? What's the matter? What's wrong with ....? What's the matter with ....? How's ......?

1) A: What's wrong with you?/What's the matter with you?
B: I've got a cold.
翻譯：A：你怎麼了？
　　　　B：我感冒了。

2) A: How's your mother?
B: She's worse than yesterday.
A: I'm sorry to hear that. Don't worry too much. She'll get better soon.
翻譯：A：令堂狀況如何。
　　　　B：她比昨天更糟了。
　　　　A：我聽了很遺憾。不用太擔心。她很快就會好一些。

4) A: What's the matter?
B: I can't find my car key.
翻譯：A：發生甚麼事？
　　　　B：我找不到汽車鑰匙。

10. 詢問 (Inquiries)

常用字詞有：How, when, where, who, why, what

1) A: Excuse me, how can I get to the railway station?
B: Take a No. 41 bus.
翻譯：A：對不起，要如何到火車站去？
　　　　B：搭 41 號公車。

2) A: Excuse me. When does the next train leave for Kaohsuing?
B: 10 a.m.

翻譯：A：對不起。去高雄的下一班火車是甚麼時候？

B：上午十點。

3) A: What's the weather like today?

B: It'll rain this afternoon.

翻譯：A：今天天氣如何？

B：下午會下雨。

4) A: How far is your home from the school?

B: Five minutes by bike.

翻譯：A：你家距離學校有多遠？

B：騎單車 5 分鐘。

11. 意向 (Intentions)

常用字詞有：I'd like …, Would you like to…? What do you want …?

1) A: What do you want to be in the future?

B: I want to be a businessman.

翻譯：A：你將來想當甚麼？

B：我想當生意人。

2) A: Would you like to work at the South Pole in the future?

B: Yes, we'd love to.

翻譯：A：你將來喜歡在南極工作嗎？

B：是的，我會喜歡。

3) A: I'd like fried eggs with peas and pork, too.

B: OK.

翻譯：A：我想要豆子、豬肉炒蛋。

B：沒問題。

12. 喜歡、不喜歡/偏愛 (Likes, dislikes and preferences)

常用字詞有：like, dislike, prefer, enjoy

1) A: Which kind of apples do you prefer, red ones or green ones?

B: Green ones.

翻譯：A：你比較喜歡哪一種蘋果，紅的還是綠的？

B：綠的。

2) A: Do you enjoy music or dance?

B: I enjoy music.

翻譯：A：你喜歡音樂還是跳舞？

B：我喜歡音樂。

3) A: How did you like the play?

B: It was wonderful.

翻譯：A：這齣戲你覺得如何？

B：很棒。

13. 提供（Offers）

常用字詞有：Can I ....? Let me .... What can I ...? Would you like ...?

1) A: Can I help you?

B: Yes, please.

翻譯：A：可以幫你忙嗎？

B：是的，謝謝。

2) A: Let me help you.

B: Thanks.

翻譯：A：我來幫你忙。

B：謝謝。

3) A: Would you like a drink?

B: That's very kind of you.

翻譯：A：要來杯飲料嗎？

B：你真好意。

4) A: Shall I get a trolley for you?

B: No, thanks.

翻譯：A：要我拿輛手推車給你嗎？

B：不用，謝謝。

全新國中會考英語聽力精選 下冊
目　　錄

全新國中會考英語聽力精選(下)
Unit 1

I、Listen and choose the right picture. (根據你所聽到的內容,選出相應的圖片。)（6分）

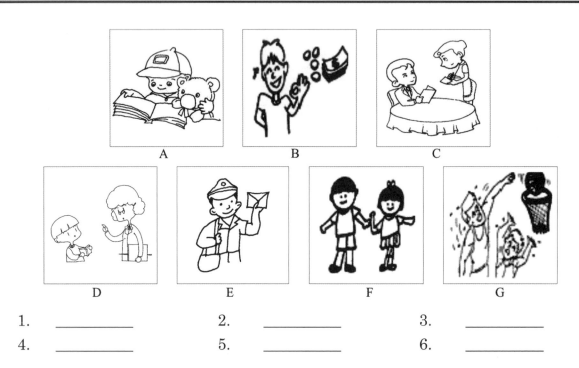

1. _____   2. _____   3. _____
4. _____   5. _____   6. _____

II、Listen to the dialogue and choose the best answer to the question. （根據你所聽到的對話和問題，選出最恰當的答案。）（10分）

( ) 7.　(A)Alice's cousin.　　　　(B)Alice's brother.
　　　　(C)Alice's sister.　　　　(D)Alice's pen-friend.

( ) 8.　(A)German.　　　　　　(B)Japanese.
　　　　(C)Korean.　　　　　　(D)Chinese.

( ) 9.　(A)In a bookstore.　　　　(B)In a library.
　　　　(C)In a hospital.　　　　(D)In a cinema.

( ) 10.　(A)When we need to make friends.　(B)Why we need to make friends.
　　　　(C)When to make friends.　　　　(D)How to make friends.

( ) 11.　(A)Monday.　　　(B)Sunday.　　　(C)Tuesday.　　　(D)Wednesday.

( ) 12.　(A)By visiting their houses.　(B)By writing ordinary mails.
　　　　(C)By writing e-mails.　　　(D)By phone.

( ) 13.　(A)By underground.(B)By taxi.

(C)By bus. (D)On foot.

( ) 14. (A)Cartoons. (B)Action movies.
(C)Horror movies. (D)Adventure movies.

( ) 15. (A)It's impossible to make real friends with so many people.
(B)In fact, the woman has no friends around her.
(C)The woman is telling a lie and she is dishonest.
(D)The man wants to tell the woman not to make many friends.

( ) 16. (A)At 8. (B)At 7:45. (C)At 7:55. (D)At 8:05.

Ⅲ、Listen to the passage and tell whether the following statements are true or false.（判斷下列句子是否符合你聽到的短文內容,符合用 T 表示,不符合用 F 表示）（7分）

( ) 17. Human beings can't do without friends.

( ) 18. The writer doesn't want her friends to come to her when she is very sad.

( ) 19. According to the writer, a real friend is the same as a precious pearl.

( ) 20. To have the same hobbies or interests is the first thing that people consider when they make friends.

( ) 21. The writer wants to make friends with those who have enough power.

( ) 22. The writer doesn't want to make friends with people who wear glasses.

( ) 23. The support the writer gives to her friend will never change all her life.

Ⅳ、Listen to the passage and fill in the blanks with proper words.（聽短文,用最恰當的填空,每格限填一詞）（共7分）

● The nationality of the pen-friend is __24__.

● Now he studies in Grade __25__ in a Junior High School.

● The subjects he does well in are __26__ and math.

● The pen-friend __27__ me to teach him Chinese at the beginning.

● He seems to have lots of __28__.

● In his letters, he shares with me many __29__ in his country.

● I hope to meet him in China so that we can __30__ with each other better.

24. _____ 25. _____ 26. _____ 27. _____

28. _____ 29. _____ 30. _____

全新國中會考英語聽力精選(下)
Unit 2

I、Listen and choose the right picture.（根據你所聽到的內容，選出相應的圖片。）（6分）

A.　　　　　　　B.　　　　　　　C.

D.　　　　　E.　　　　　F.　　　　　G.

1. ＿＿＿＿＿＿　　2. ＿＿＿＿＿＿　　3. ＿＿＿＿＿＿

4. ＿＿＿＿＿＿　　5. ＿＿＿＿＿＿　　6. ＿＿＿＿＿＿

II、Listen to the dialogue and choose the best answer to the question you hear.（根據你所聽到的對話和問題，選出最恰當的答案。）（10分）

( ) 7. (A)Before 3.15.　　(B)At 3.30.　　(C)At 3.15.　　(D)At 3.50.

( ) 8. (A)The girl's.　　　　　　　(B)The boy's.

(C)The doctor's.　　　　　(D)Someone else's.

( ) 9. (A)Chinese and physics.　　(B)English and music.

(C)History and music.　　　(D)English and history.

( ) 10. (A)By plane.　　(B)By car.　　(C)By train.　　(D)By ship.

( ) 11. (A)A manager.　　　　　(B)A businesswoman.

(C)A pilot.　　　　　　　(D)An airhostess.

（　　）12. (A)About two weeks.　　　　　　　　(B)About three weeks.
　　　　　 (C)About four weeks.　　　　　　　 (D)About five weeks.

（　　）13. (A)At 2.55.　　(B)At 1.55.　　(C)At 2.40.　　(D)At 1.40.

（　　）14. (A)In a library.　　　　　　　　　 (B)In a book shop.
　　　　　 (C)In a reading room.　　　　　　 (D)In the man's home.

（　　）15. (A)By bus.　　(B)By bike.　　(C)By underground. (D)By train.

（　　）16. (A)No, he can't.　　(B)Yes, he can.　　(C)No, he couldn't.　　(D)Yes, he could.

Ⅲ、Listen to the passage and decide whether the following statements are True (T) or False (F). （判斷下列句子是否符合你所聽到的短文內容，符合的用 T 表示，不符合的用 F 表示。）（7分）

（　　）17. Angela has got a penfriend in Australia.

（　　）18. Spring in Canberra lasts for about four months.

（　　）19. Summer in Canberra usually starts at the beginning of February.

（　　）20. Judy enjoys going to the sea in summer.

（　　）21. Judy doesn't talk much about autumn in Canberra in her letter.

（　　）22. Winter in Canberra is always rainy and cold.

（　　）23. Judy's favourite season is spring.

Ⅳ、Listen to the passage and fill in the blanks. （根據你聽到的短文，完成下列內容，每空格限填一詞。）（7分）

- Anita __24__ up at 6 a.m.
- After doing some washing, she __25__ English for half an hour.
- At 26, she has breakfast.
- At 8 a.m., she __27__ to school.
- At 4 p.m., she __28__ home.
- At __29__, she begins to do her homework.
- At 9 p.m., she goes to __30__.

24. _____　　25. _____　　26. _____　　27. _____

28. _____　　29. _____　　30. _____

全新國中會考英語聽力精選(下)
Unit 3

I、Listen and choose the right picture. (根據你所聽到的內容，選出相應的圖片。) (6分)

A.

B.

C.

D.

E.

F.

G.

1. _____   2. _____   3. _____

4. _____   5. _____   6. _____

II、Listen to the dialogue and choose the best answer to the question you hear. (根據你所聽到的對話和問題，選出最恰當的答案。) (10分)

( ) 7. (A)At the corner of the street.   (B)At the end of the street.
        (C)At the No. 48 bus stop.   (D)The lady has no idea.

( ) 8. (A)A blue handbag.   (B)A brown handbag.
        (C)13 dollars.   (D)30 dollars.

( ) 9. (A)Physics.   (B)English.   (C)Maths.   (D)Chemistry.

( ) 10. (A)A No. 49 bus.   (B)The bus stop.   (C)The post office.   (D)A street.

( ) 11. (A)John and Ellen.   (B)Miss Gray and Mrs Smith.
        (C)Mr Smith and Miss Gray.   (D)John and Gray.

(　　) 12. (A)He watched TV at home.　　　　(B)He went to see a film.
　　　　　　(C)He visited the photo show.　　　　(D)He visited the flower show.

(　　) 13. (A)She gave it to Jim.　　　　　　(B)She put it on the desk.
　　　　　　(C)She put it in the desk drawer　　(D)She didn't see it.

(　　) 14. (A)Because the restaurant is new.　　(B)Because they enjoy fast food.
　　　　　　(C)Because the food there is not expensive.
　　　　　　(D)Because they are hungry and want to have lunch there.

(　　) 15. (A)By train.　　　　　　　　　　(B)By plane.
　　　　　　(C)In about two hours.　　　　　(D)Before three o'clock.

(　　) 16. (A)America.　　(B)Australia.　　(C)France.　　(D)Japan.

Ⅲ、Listen to the passage and decide whether the following statements are True (T) or False (F). （判斷下列句子是否符合你所聽到的短文內容，符合的用 T 表示，不符合的用 F 表示。）（7分）

(　　) 17. There is a lecture on Wednesday evening and another lecture on Thursday evening.

(　　) 18. The Wednesday's lecture is about how to protect eyesight.

(　　) 19. Nancy is sure that Henry will be glad to listen to the lecture.

(　　) 20. Nancy was late for the lecture.

(　　) 21. The ticket-collector was a very kind man.

(　　) 22. Nancy and Henry are not allowed to enter because they are late.

(　　) 23. It seems that Nancy doesn't remember things very well.

Ⅳ、Listen to the passage and fill in the blanks. （根據你聽到的短文，完成下列內容，每空格限填一詞。）（7分）

- Someone sent Eddie a long and __24__ package with pink paper outside. It was an __25__.

- Someone sent Eddie a square package with __26__ paper outside and a book inside.

- Eddie also received a globe of the world packed in a big, __27__ package with yellow paper from his __28__.

- Eddie received a portable computer packed with __29__ boxes in green, red and blue paper from his __30__.

24. _____　　25. _____　　26. _____　　27. _____
28. _____　　29. _____　　30. _____

全新國中會考英語聽力精選(下)

Unit 4

I、Listen and choose the right picture.（根據你所聽到的內容,選出相應的圖片。）（6分）

A

B

C

D

E

F

G

1. ＿＿＿＿＿＿　　2. ＿＿＿＿＿＿　　3. ＿＿＿＿＿＿

4. ＿＿＿＿＿＿　　5. ＿＿＿＿＿＿　　6. ＿＿＿＿＿＿

II、Listen to the dialogue and choose the best answer to the question. （根據你所聽到的對話和問題，選出最恰當的答案。）（10分）

(　) 7.　(A)16.　(B)40.　(C)22.　(D)18.

(　) 8.　(A)7:50.　(B)10:50.　(C)9:30.　(D)11:50.

(　) 9.　(A)For 13 days.　(B)For 2 weeks.　(C)For 6 days.　(D)For 7 days.

(　) 10.　(A)8.　(B)6.　(C)3.　(D)7.

(　) 11.　(A)10 yuan.　(B)99 yuan.　(C)90 yuan.　(D)100 yuan.

(　) 12.　(A)25 min.　(B)35 min.　(C)15 min.　(D)20 min.

(　) 13.　(A)61213009.　(B)62131009.　(C)62131008.　(D)61213008.

(　) 14.　(A)1 liter.　(B)2 liters.　(C)0.5 liter.　(D)0.25 liter.

(　) 15.　(A)4.　(B)5.　(C)3.　(D)6.

(　) 16.　(A)March 1st.　(B)Feb. 29rd.　(C)Feb. 28th.　(D)Feb. 27th.

III、Listen to the passage and tell whether the following statements are true or false. （判

( ) 17. In the writer's opinion, one is an unlucky number.

( ) 18. The earthquake that happened in Taiwan in 2001 killed about 2,000 people.

( ) 19. The terrorists attacked the U.S. on 9·11 because they thought one was really a bad number.

( ) 20. The airplanes crashed into the tall buildings and luckily flew back to the air base.

( ) 21. On 7·11, a big typhoon attacked Taiwan in 2001.

( ) 22. Some people died in the typhoon because the wind took them away.

( ) 23. According to the writer, January has the most days on which he will be quite careful.

IV、Listen to the passage and fill in the blanks with proper words.（聽短文,用最恰當的填空,每格限填一詞）（共 7 分）

- A serious earthquake hit New Zealand at around __24__ a.m. local time.

- Christchurch, New Zealand's second-largest city has a population of about __25__ people.

- The U.S. Geological Survey at first reported it at 7.4 but later changed its figure to __26__.

- The quake lasted up to __27__ seconds.

- About __28__ earthquakes happen in New Zealand every year.

- The last serious earthquake in New Zealand took place in __29__.

- __30__ people lost their lives in the last serious earthquake.

24. _____   25. _____   26. _____   27. _____

28. _____   29. _____   30. _____

全新國中會考英語聽力精選(下)
Unit 5

A   B   C

D   E   F   G

1. _____   2. _____   3. _____
4. _____   5. _____   6. _____

Ⅰ、Listen and choose the best response to the sentence you hear.（根據你所聽到的句子,選出最恰當的應答句。）（6分）

( ) 7.   (A)A direction sign. (B)An information sign.
          (C)An instruction sign.   (D)A warning sign.

( ) 8.   (A)Sorry, you mustn't.   (B)Yes, you may.
          (C)There are flowers in the park.   (D)Flowers are nice.

( ) 9.   (A)I will take your advice.   (B)That's good.
          (C)You should study harder.   (D)I think so.

( ) 10.   (A)Thank you.   (B)Don't say so.
          (C)No, I don't.   (D)That's all right.

( ) 11.   (A)Good idea.   (B)I think so, too.
          (C)Yes, I will.   (D)I'm glad.

（　）12.　(A)For at least one hour. (B)In one hour.
　　　　　　(C)At one o'clock. (D)By one hour.

Ⅲ、Listen to the dialogue and choose the best answer to the question you hear.（根據你所聽到的對話和問題,選出最恰當的答案。）（6分）

（　）13.　(A)Yes, he can. (B)No, he can't.
　　　　　　(C)Yes, he does. (D)No, he doesn't.

（　）14.　(A)At home. (B)In the hospital.
　　　　　　(C)At the zoo. (D)In the reading room.

（　）15.　(A)An SPCA officer. (B)Homeless children.
　　　　　　(C)Homeless animals. (D)Three years ago.

（　）16.　(A)10. (B)15.
　　　　　　(C)20. (D)25.

（　）17.　(A)A police officer. (B)To catch thieves.
　　　　　　(C)To help others. (D)A doctor.

（　）18.　(A)Wednesday. (B)Thursday.
　　　　　　(C)Tuesday. (D)Friday.

Ⅳ、Listen to the dialogue and decide whether the following statements are True (T) or False (F).（判斷下列句子內容是否符合你所聽到的對話內容,符合的用"T"表示,不符合的用"F"表示。）（6分）

（　）19.　Mr and Mrs White went to the city centre on Saturday.

（　）20.　When Mr and Mrs White returned home late, it was very dark in the room.

（　）21.　Mr and Mrs White's bedroom is on the ground floor.

（　）22.　On the way to the front door, they heard someone talking.

（　）23.　Two boys broke into the house during the day time and stayed there.

（　）24.　Mr White forgot to turn off the TV in the morning.

25. Good study habits are very _____.

26. When you have good study habits, you learn things _____.

27. When you study, don't think about _____ things at the same time.

28. If you do this, you will make _____ mistakes.

29. Every student should _____ good habits.

30. If your study habits are already good, try to make them _____.

全新國中會考英語聽力精選(下)

Unit 6

I、Listen and choose the right picture.（根據你所聽到的內容，選出相應的圖片。）（6分）

A.	B.	C.

D.	E.	F.	G.

1. _____ 2. _____ 3. _____

4. _____ 5. _____ 6. _____

II、Listen to the dialogue and choose the best answer to the question you hear.（根據你所聽到的對話和問題，選出最恰當的答案。）（10分）

（　）7. (A)At 5.45a.m.　(B)At 6.15a.m.　(C)At 6.45a.m.　(D)At 6.55a.m.

（　）8. (A)　　　　(B)　　　　(C)　　　　(D)

（　）9. (A)Because she was late for the bus.　(B)Because the picnic is terrible.
　　　　(C)Because the TV play is interesting.　(D)Because it was raining hard.

（　）10. (A)Yes, both of them liked it.
　　　　(B)No, neither of them liked it.
　　　　(C)His father didn't like it, but his mother did.
　　　　(D)His mother didn't like it, but his father did.

( ) 11. (A)To have some fish.　　　　　　(B)To have some meat.
　　　 (C)To have some vegetables.　　　 (D)To have some chicken.

( ) 12. (A)He has been to the city centre before.
　　　 (B)He is too busy.
　　　 (C)He doesn't like the city center.
　　　 (D)He will not go to the city center.

( ) 13. (A)At home.　　　　　　　　　　(B)In the hospital.
　　　 (C)In the library.　　　　　　　　(D)On the playground.

( ) 14. (A)She has a cold.　　　　　　　　(B)She has toothache.
　　　 (C)She has a cough.　　　　　　　(D)She has a stomachache.

( ) 15. (A)By bus.　　　(B)By train.　　　(C)By plane.　　　(D)By ship.

( ) 16. (A)Teacher and student.　　　　　(B)Husband and wife.
　　　 (C)Father and daughter.　　　　　(D)Mother and son.

Ⅲ、Listen to the passage and tell whether the following statements are true or false. (判斷下列句子是否符合你所聽到的短文內容, 符合的用"T"表示，不符合的用"F"表示。) (7分)

( ) 17. Stephen Hawking was born in Oxford and once studied in Cambridge University.

( ) 18. As a university student, Stephen Hawking worked hard and got good marks.

( ) 19. Stephen Hawking first noticed something was wrong with him when he was 23.

( ) 20. Stephen Hawking changed his life attitude after he came out of the hospital.

( ) 21. Later Stephen Hawking married and there were three people in his family.

( ) 22. Stephen Hawking did some scientific researches and now works as a professor at Oxford University.

( ) 23. From the passage, we know that we shouldn't lose hope even in a bad situation.

Ⅳ、Listen to the passage and fill in the blanks. (根據你聽到的短文，完成下列內容，每空格限填一詞。) (7分)

● Marco Daniel wants some information about the __24__ club.

● The members in the club meet every __25__ evening.

- Matches on Sunday morning are just for their __26__ players.

- The meetings begin at __27__, and are about two hours long.

- People like to get home before 10:15 to watch the __28__ program on TV.

- They meet in the Jubilee Hall in Park Lane, behind __29__ Street.

- The hall doesn't have very good heating, so Marco Daniel should take a __30__ to put on afterwards.

24. _____   25. _____   26. _____   27. _____

28. _____   29. _____   30. _____

全新國中會考英語聽力精選(下)

Unit 7

I、Listen and choose the right picture. (根據你所聽到的內容，選出相應的圖片。)(6分)

A.　　　　　　　B.　　　　　　　C.

D.　　　　E.　　　　F.　　　　G.

1. _____　　2. _____　　3. _____

4. _____　　5. _____　　6. _____

II、Listen to the dialogue and choose the best answer to the question you hear. (根據你所聽到的對話和問題，選出最恰當的答案。)(10分)

(　) 7. (A)Maths.　　　(B)Sports.　　　(C)Music.　　　(D)Science.

(　) 8. (A)Tom wants to do it by himself.　　(B)Tom doesn't think it's so hard.
　　　　(C)Tom is very clever.　　(D)His mother can't work it out.

(　) 9. (A)At the school.　　(B)At the school library.
　　　　(C)On the playground.　　(D)At home.

(　) 10. (A)The man got a new receipt.　　(B)The man got his radio repaired.
　　　　(C)The man got a new radio.　　(D)The man left there without a radio.

(　) 11. (A)Mike.　　(B)Mike's mother.　　(C)Mike's sister.　　(D)Mike's father.

(　) 12. (A)Before class. (B)During the class.
(C)After class. (D)In the classroom.

(　) 13. (A)By bus. (B)By bike. (C)By car. (D)On foot.

(　) 14. (A)Five minutes. (B)Fifteen minutes.
(C)Twenty minutes. (D)Twenty-five minutes.

(　) 15. (A)We don't know from this passage. (B)The girl.
(C)Wang Pen. (D)Li Ming.

(　) 16. (A)She's too busy to go. (B)She's not interested in it.
(C)She hasn't got any tickets. (D)She's ill.

Ⅲ、Listen to the passage and decide whether the following statements are True (T) or False (F). (判斷下列句子內容是否符合你所聽到的短文內容，符合的用 T 表示，不符合的用 F 表示。)（7分）

(　) 17. Kelly always wanted to be an astronaut to work in space one day.

(　) 18. Kelly always thought that she would discover some important things in the future.

(　) 19. One night, Kelly saw a strange, coloured light moving across the sky in the park with her dog.

(　) 20. Kelly thought the light was from a spaceship.

(　) 21. The spaceship landed a few metres in front of Kelly.

(　) 22. Kelly was able to understand what the aliens in the spaceship said.

(　) 23. Kelly's dog went up to the spaceship and never came back again.

Ⅳ、Listen to the dialogue and fill in the blanks. (根據你聽到的對話，完成下列內容，每空格限填一詞。)（7分）

People will live on the __24__. They will also live in __25__ houses by the year 2100.
__26__ will cure every illness in the future and people will live __27__ than ever.
People will have __28__ in space and live on other __29__.
People will run out of energy sources in the future so people must try to protect the __30__.

24. _____　　25. _____　　26. _____　　27. _____

28. _____　　29. _____　　30. _____

全新國中會考英語聽力精選(下)

Unit 8

A.　　　　　　　　B.　　　　　　　　C.

D.　　　　　　　　E.　　　　　　　　F.

1.＿＿＿＿＿

2.＿＿＿＿＿

3.＿＿＿＿＿

4.＿＿＿＿＿

5.＿＿＿＿＿

Ⅱ、Listen and choose the right word you hear in each sentence.（根據你所聽到的句子，選出正確的單字。）（5分）

( ) 6.　(A)meet　　　(B)meat　　　(C)met　　　(D)meeting

( ) 7.　(A)friend　　(B)fry　　　(C)fried　　　(D)frog

( ) 8.　(A)seventy　(B)seven　　(C)seventeen　(D)seventh

( ) 9.　(A)prize　　(B)praise　　(C)please　　(D)price

( ) 10.　(A)soup　　(B)soap　　(C)supper　　(D)super

Ⅲ、Listen and choose the best response to the sentence you hear.（根據你所聽到的句子，選出最恰當的應答句。）（5分）

( ) 11.　(A)Yes, I would like some rice.

　　　　(B)Yes, I would like some noodles.

　　　　(C)I don't want any dumplings.

　　　　(D)Rice, please.

( ) 12.　(A)In the supermarket, at the meat section.

　　　　(B)In the supermarket, at the frozen food section.

(C)In the market, in the seafood stall.

(D)In the market, in the fruit stall.

( ) 13. (A)24 yuan altogether. (B)I bought a box of apples.

(C)I don't like apples at all. (D)Let's have some apples.

( ) 14. (A)That's a good idea. (B)Thank you very much.

(C)Nice to meet you.(D)Let's go to the supermarket.

( ) 15. (A)I have bought some ice cream in the supermarket.

(B)I have bought two boxes of ice cream.

(C)I have bought my daughter some ice cream.

(D)I bought the ice cream yesterday.

IV、Listen to the dialogue and choose the best answer to the question you hear. （根據你所聽到的對話和問題，選出最恰當的答案。）（5分）

( ) 16. (A)Water. (B)Cola. (C)Coffee. (D)Tea.

( ) 17. (A)￥45. (B)￥57. (C)￥37. (D)￥75.

( ) 18. (A)Meat section. (B)Seafood section.

(C)Drink section. (D)Frozen food section.

( ) 19. (A)Mango ice cream. (B)Mango pudding.

(C)Strawberry ice cream. (D)Strawberry pudding.

( ) 20. (A)A pizza café. (B)A fast food restaurant.

(C)The KFC. (D)A Chinese restaurant.

V、Listen to the passage and decide whether the following statements are True (T) or False (F). （判斷下列句子內容是否符合你所聽到的短文內容，符合的用 T 表示，不符合的用 F 表示。）（5分）

( ) 21. Pizza is very popular in the world.

( ) 22. The name of the world's first pizza restaurant is Naples.

( ) 23. The first modern pizza was made more than 100 years ago.

( ) 24. The first modern pizza looked like the Italian national flag.

( ) 25. People can only order pizza in a pizza café.

Wendy's Café

1. Sandwiches（with）
☐ Chicken ￥6.50　　☐ Beef　￥7.50　　☐ Ham　￥5.00

2. Meat/Seafood
☐ Fried chicken wings　￥20.00　　☐ Steamed prawns with garlic　￥35.00

3. Soup
☐ Tomato and egg soup　￥6.00　　☐ Tomato soup　￥5.00
☐ Cabbage soup with beef　￥10.00　　☐ Fish soup　￥10.00

4. Salad
☐ Vegetable salad　￥5.00 ☐ Fruit salad　￥5.00☐

5. Drinks
☐ Coffee　￥5.00　　☐ Tea　￥4.00　　☐ Apple juice　￥4.00

26. _____　　27. _____　　28. _____

29. _____　　30. _____

全新國中會考英語聽力精選(下)

Unit 9

I、Listen and choose the right picture. （根據你所聽到的內容,選出相應的圖片。）（6分）

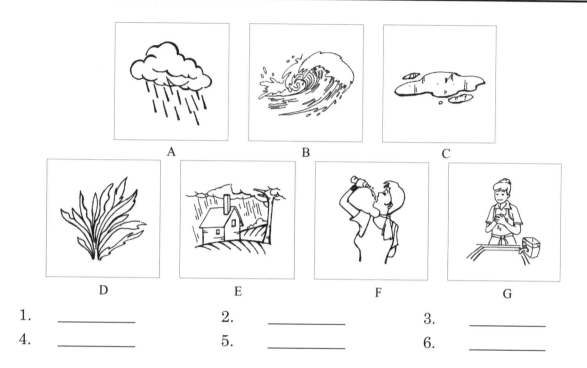

A	B	C

D	E	F	G

1. _____   2. _____   3. _____

4. _____   5. _____   6. _____

II、Listen to the dialogue and choose the best answer to the question. （根據你所聽到的對話和問題，選出最恰當的答案。）（10分）

（   ）7.　(A)Water.　　　(B)Coffee.　　　(C)Tea.　　　(D)Wine.

（   ）8.　(A)18 dollars.　(B)80 dollars.　(C)480 dollars.　(D)108 dollars.

（   ）9.　(A)Turn off the tap. (B)Use less water.
　　　　　(C)Educate those who waste water.　(D)Tell others to drink less.

（   ）10.　(A)Seeing the doctor.　　　　　(B)Cooking.
　　　　　(C)Having dinner.　　　　　　　(D)Lying in bed.

（   ）11.　(A)Basketball.　　　　　　　(B)Swimming.
　　　　　(C)Tennis.　　　　　　　　　(D)Football.

（   ）12.　(A)She doesn't want to send an email.
　　　　　(B)She has been controlled by the computer.
　　　　　(C)Her parents asked her to write on the paper.
　　　　　(D)She is not allowed to use the computer.

( ) 13. (A)In the U.K. (B)In the U.S.A.
(C)In the P.R.C. (D)In the U.N.

( ) 14. (A)A movie. (B)A book. (C)A magazine. (D)A story.

( ) 15. (A)She ate much spicy food. (B)She liked eating too much.
(C)She didn't have her breakfast. (D)She was not feeling well.

( ) 16. (A)She wants the boy never to be late again.
(B)She isn't angry with the boy.
(C)She wants the boy never to come to the fair.
(D)She doesn't care about the boy.

Ⅲ、Listen to the passage and tell whether the following statements are true or false. （判斷下列句子是否符合你听到的短文內容,符合用 T 表示,不符合用 F 表示）（7 分）

( ) 17. Yellowstone is the first park in America and even in the world.

( ) 18. Yellowstone has been open for more than 130 years.

( ) 19. There are no cages in Yellowstone, but animals are unable to live in a natural way.

( ) 20. Animals in Yellowstone are quite happy if people feed food to them.

( ) 21. Hunting animals in Yellowstone will bring damage to animals' life.

( ) 22. People and wild animals live together peacefully in Yellowstone.

( ) 23. In most zoos, animals are kept in cages.

Ⅳ、Listen to the passage and fill in the blanks with proper words. (聽短文,用最恰當的填空,每格限填一詞)（共 7 分）

- Rivers, as a kind of __24__ resources, are quite important.
- At least one river __25__ through a country and it plays an important role.
- The Nile is the longest river worldwide and is the lifeline of __26__.
- Large ships can go about thousands of miles upon the Amazon because it is so __27__ and wide.
- Rivers also give food, water to drink, water to irrigate __28__, and chances for fun.
- The problem of river pollution is __29__ by chemicals and other materials from large cities or industries located upon rivers.
- Keeping rivers clean can make human beings enjoy the __30__ of this natural resource.

24. _____   25. _____   26. _____   27. _____
28. _____   29. _____   30. _____

全新國中會考英語聽力精選(下)
Unit 10

I、Listen and choose the right picture. (根據你所聽到的內容，選出相應的圖片。)(6分)

A.　　　　　B.　　　　　C.

D.　　　　　E.　　　　　F.　　　　　G.

1. _____　　2. _____　　3. _____

4. _____　　5. _____　　6. _____

II、Listen and choose the best response to the sentence you hear. (根據你所聽到的句子，選出最恰當的應答句。)(6分)

( ) 7.　(A)Who are you?　　　　　　(B)This is Ben speaking.
　　　(C)Is that Ben?　　　　　　(D)Are you Ben speaking?

( ) 8.　(A)Whose idea?　　　　　　(B)Sounds terrible!
　　　(C)That sounds great.　　　(D)I won't go with you.

( ) 9.　(A)See you then.　　　　　(B)I have no time.
　　　(C)I will go by myself.　　(D)Thank you very much.

( ) 10.　(A)Oh, it sounds great.　(B)Have a great dream.
　　　(C)Have a good time.　　(D)Oh, what a pity!

(　　) 11.　(A)We need some eggs, some sugar, some butter, some flour and some chocolate powder.

(B)We have to go to the supermarket to buy these things.

(C)We need to buy some eggs, some flour and some chocolate powder first.

(D)Can you show me how to bake a chocolate cake?

(　　) 12.　(A)No. We don't need any food.　(B)Let's have some spicy sausages!

(C)Are there any soft drinks?　(D)I can't agree with you.

Ⅲ、Listen to the dialogue and choose the best answer to the question you hear.（根據你所聽到的對話和問題，選出最恰當的答案。）（6分）

(　　) 13.　(A)Tomorrow is Eddie's birthday.

(B)There is going to be a surprise birthday party.

(C)Eddie won't go to the birthday party.

(D)John will have a surprise birthday present from Eddie.

(　　) 14.　(A)John doesn't like hot dogs.　(B)John likes dogs.

(C)Sandra will give John a puppy.　(D)Eddie will give John a hot dog.

(　　) 15.　(A)Fried fish finger. (B)Fried rice.

(C)Chicken.　(D)KFC.

(　　) 16.　(A)Sugar.　(B)Icing sugar.　(C)Chocolate.　(D)Eggs.

(　　) 17.　(A)At the party.　(B)Before the party.

(C)After the party.　(D)We don't know.

(　　) 18.　(A)6.25.　(B)6.40.　(C)6.55.　(D)7.00.

Ⅳ、Listen to the dialogue and decide whether the following statements are True (T) or False (F).（判斷下列句子內容是否符合你所聽到的對話內容，符合的用"T" 表示，不符合的用"F" 表示。）（6分）

(　　) 19.　It was Tommy's eleventh birthday party.

(　　) 20.　There were no captions on the back of the photos.

(　　) 21.　They sang karaoke that day.

(　　) 22.　They watched some cartoons.

(　　) 23.　They had a cake made by Tommy's mother.

(　　) 24.　Tommy and his friends had a good time that day.

V、Listen and fill in the blanks.（根據你所聽到的內容，用適當的單詞完成下面的句子。每空格限填一詞。）（6分）

- The world's first pizza __25__ is in Naples, a famous city in Italy.
- The pizza had the same colours as the Italian national __26__.
- The pizza had red __27__, white cheese and green herb.
- We can order chicken pizza, vegetable pizza, seafood pizza or __28__ pizza in a pizza café.
- We can also order a pizza by making a phone call at home or in the __29__.
- People can choose any __30__ they want.

25. _____   26. _____   27. _____

28. _____   29. _____   30. _____

全新國中會考英語聽力精選(下)
Unit 11

I、Listen and choose the right picture.（根據你所聽到的內容,選出相應的圖片。）（6分）

1. _____   2. _____   3. _____
4. _____   5. _____   6. _____

II、Listen to the dialogue and choose the best answer to the question. （根據你所聽到的對話和問題，選出最恰當的答案。）（10分）

( ) 7.   (A)Every day.   (B)Once a week.
          (C)Twice a month.   (D)Every month.

( ) 8.   (A)Because his teacher wanted to borrow the newspapers.
          (B)Because reading newspapers is his favorite activity.
          (C)Because it is his homework.
          (D)Because he is looking for someone he wants to meet.

( ) 9.   (A)At 3:30.   (B)At 4:00.
          (C)At 3:00.   (D)She didn't get the newspaper.

( ) 10.   (A)At a drug store.   (B)In the boy's home.
          (C)In a reading room.   (D)In a dining room.

( ) 11.   (A)Watching TV.   (B)Reading a newspaper.
          (C)Listening to the radio.   (D)Chatting on the Internet.

( ) 12. (A)Take some medicine. (B)Have a break.
(C)Speak more. (D)Go to the doctor's.

( ) 13. (A)The man agrees with the woman.
(B)The man thinks it is impossible for the woman to win.
(C)The man disagrees with the woman.
(D)The man thinks actions speak louder than words.

( ) 14. (A)In the pencil-box. (B)On the shelf.
(C)On the desk. (D)In a wooden box.

( ) 15. (A)A big balcony. (B)A study.
(C)Three bathrooms. (D)A small bathroom.

( ) 16. (A)She is good at English. (B)She likes writing diaries.
(C)She enjoys writing songs. (D)She sings English songs well.

Ⅲ、Listen to the passage and tell whether the following statements are true or false. （判斷下列句子是否符合你听到的短文内容,符合用 T 表示,不符合用 F 表示）（7分）

( ) 17. Bill studied in Grade Nine and had to go to school very early.

( ) 18. Newspapers are sent to the corner at midnight by truck.

( ) 19. Bill's customers were pleased with Bill's job.

( ) 20. Bill saved all the money he earned as a newspaper boy for college expenses.

( ) 21. Sometimes Bill's father helped him send newspapers to people.

( ) 22. Bill was a boy who might enjoy listening to music.

( ) 23. If Bill won a new bike instead of a trip to Europe, he would feel disappointed.

Ⅳ、Listen to the passage and fill in the blanks with proper words. （聽短文,用最恰當的填空,每格限填一詞）（共 7 分）

- A newspaper reporter will __24__ different kinds of people in the job.
- A reporter may have a __25__ job after looking for news everywhere for some years.
- A reporter's job ranges from covering a __26__ area to a special one.
- A reporter writes book reviews after reading the __27__ books.
- A reporter always watches movies __28__ movies are on at cinemas.
- A group of tough guys __29__ a reporter's camera when they were taken pictures of 3 years ago.

● A reporter's job is both exciting and dangerous but never ever __30__.

24. _____   25. _____   26. _____   27. _____

28. _____   29. _____   30. _____

Ⅰ、Listen and choose the right picture.（根據你所聽到的內容，選出相應的圖片。）（6分）

A.   B.   C.

D.   E.   F.   G.

1. _____ 2. _____ 3. _____
4. _____ 5. _____ 6. _____

Ⅱ、Listen and choose the best response to the sentence you hear.（根據你所聽到的句子，選出最恰當的應答句。）（6分）

( ) 7. (A)I don't like it.
      (B)It's about a swan princess and a prince.
      (C)It's a love story.
      (D)It's very exciting.

( ) 8. (A)That's interesting.   (B)They like adventures.
      (C)So do I.   (D)Neither do I.

(　) 9.　(A)OK. Let's see Swan Lake.

　　　　(B)I'm afraid I don't like stories about cowboys.

　　　　(C)It's a great cartoon.

　　　　(D)No, that's too bad.

(　) 10.　(A)Sorry, I'm new here.

　　　　(B)Yes, I can.

　　　　(C)No, you can't.

　　　　(D)You'll find the cinema on your right.

(　) 11.　(A)I like watching cartoons.

　　　　(B)The cartoon is on Channel 4.

　　　　(C)We usually watch cartoons at weekends.

　　　　(D)Yes, but the music is too noisy.

(　) 12.　(A)That's all right.　　　　　　　(B)I won't.

　　　　(C)All right.　　　　　　　　　　(D)Thank you.

Ⅲ、Listen to the dialogue and choose the best answer to the question you hear.（根據你所聽到的對話和問題，選出最恰當的答案。）（6分）

(　) 13.　(A)Swimming.　　(B)Tennis.　　(C)Volleyball.　　(D)Football.

(　) 14.　(A)In the bedroom.　　　　　　(B)At school.

　　　　(C)In the hospital.　　　　　　(D)At a cinema.

(　) 15.　(A)By taxi.　　　　　　　　　　(B)By car.

　　　　(C)By bus.　　　　　　　　　　(D)By underground.

(　) 16.　(A)Action films.　(B)Love stories.　(C)Funny films.　(D)Cartoons.

(　) 17.　(A)It's fine.　　(B)It's raining.　(C)It's cloudy.　(D)It's windy.

(　) 18.　(A)No. 2.　　　(B)No. 22.　　(C)No. 21.　　(D)No. 12.

Ⅳ、Listen to the passage and decide whether the following statements are True (T) or False (F).（判斷下列句子內容是否符合你所聽到的短文內容，符合的用"T"表示，不符合的用"F"表示。）（6分）

(　) 19.　The average American family has the TV on for more than 7 hours every day.

(　) 20.　Children watch too much television.

(　) 21.　TV-Turnoff Network is asking people not to watch TV.

(　) 22.　In 2002 TV-Turnoff Network got a lot of people to stop watching TV forever.

(　) 23.　Some Hollywood stars think it's a good idea to watch less TV.

(   ) 24.   Tom Cruise allows his children to watch TV for 3.5 hours every day.

V、Listen to the passage and complete the table.（根據你所聽到的短文內容，用適當的單詞或數字完成下面的表格。每空格限填一詞或數字。）（6分）

Film: Red Cliff	Price: __25__ yuan
Where: Yonghua 26	When: Ends on __27__ Aug.
How long: __28__ minutes	Director: __29__ Woo
Show time: 6.30 p.m.; __30__ p.m.; 9.30 p.m.	

25. _____   26. _____   27. _____

28. _____   29. _____   30. _____

Unit 13

1. _____
4. _____
2. _____
5. _____
3. _____
6. _____

II、Listen to the dialogue and choose the best answer to the question. （根據你所聽到的對話和問題，選出最恰當的答案。）（10 分）

( ) 7.　(A)Visit her aunt.　　　　(B)See her grandma.
　　　　(C)Watch the show　　　　(D)Go to the park.

( ) 8.　(A)Math and physics.　　　(B)Physics and Chinese.
　　　　(C)English and math.　　　(D)English and Chinese.

( ) 9.　(A)Next Monday.　　　　　(B)Next Friday.
　　　　(C)Next Wednesday.　　　 (D)Next Thursday.

( ) 10.　(A)By metro.　　　　　　 (B)By taxi.
　　　　 (C)By car.　　　　　　　 (D)On foot.

( ) 11.　(A)The woman with long hair is 37 years old.
　　　　 (B)The woman with short hair is a teacher.
　　　　 (C)The class teacher of Class Ten has long hair.
　　　　 (D)The class teacher of Class Four is 37 years old.

( ) 12.　(A)In a bookstore.　　　　(B)At the bank.
　　　　 (C)In the post office.　　 (D)In a museum.

( ) 13.　(A)13815273749.　　　　　(B)13817253749.
　　　　 (C)13817273549.　　　　　(D)13817273745.

(   ) 14.   (A)94 points.   (B)96 points.
                 (C)98 points.   (D)100 points.

(   ) 15.   (A)How to study well.   (B)Super stars.
                 (C)A TV program.   (D)Daily news.

(   ) 16.   (A)England.   (B)France.
                 (C)America.   (D)Germany.

Ⅲ、Listen to the passage and tell whether the following statements are true or false.（判斷下列句子是否符合你听到的短文內容,符合用 T 表示,不符合用 F 表示）（7分）

(   ) 17.   A young traveler lost his way on the Alps.

(   ) 18.   An old man with magic power saved the traveler's life.

(   ) 19.   The old man used a metal pipe to dig a hole where the seed could be put.

(   ) 20.   The old man lived alone and wanted to do something useful.

(   ) 21.   The traveler came to the place again twenty years later.

(   ) 22.   The wasteland disappeared and the land looked beautiful and smelt nice.

(   ) 23.   The writer saw the 100,000 trees and was thankful to the old man.

Ⅳ、Listen to the passage and fill in the blanks with proper words.（聽短文,用最恰當的填空,每格限填一詞）（共7分）

● In Japan, a new electronic __24__ book has appeared.

● The books tell where you are, the history of landmarks and buildings, and the shopping __25__ of the city.

● All the buildings, shops, neon lights and __26__ streets around you make you confused in Japan.

● The electronic book looks like a smart __27__ in appearance.

● Travelers as well as __28__ people can have some fun with the newly-produced book.

● The book is more useful and __29__ than a normal map.

● What the system __30__ is "Anyone, any time, anywhere".

24. _____   25. _____   26. _____   27. _____

28. _____   29. _____   30. _____

Unit 14

I、Listen and choose the right picture.（根據你所聽到的內容,選出相應的圖片。）（6分）

A   B   C

D   E   F   G

1. _____   2. _____   3. _____

4. _____   5. _____   6. _____

II、Listen and choose the best response to the sentence you hear.（根據你所聽到的句子,選出最恰當的應答句。）（6分）

（　）7.   (A)I'm Jenny.   (B)Yes, I am.
            (C)Sorry, she isn't here.   (D)Who are you?

（　）8.   (A)We are friends.   (B)We are fine. Thanks.
            (C)We have been to Japan.   (D)We will stay at home.

（　）9.   (A)After three days.(B)At midnight.
            (C)Three days later.   (D)Since three days.

（　）10.   (A)I've lost my key rings.   (B)I'm 15 years old.
            (C)I will buy a new shirt.   (D)I am right.

（　）11.   (A)To Beijing.   (B)100 yuan.
            (C)At five in the afternoon.   (D)It's for sale.

(   ) 12.   (A)Bye bye.   (B)Hello. Nice to meet you.
          (C)What's your name?   (D)Who's your friend?

Ⅲ、Listen to the dialogue and choose the best answer to the question you hear. （根據你
    所聽到的對話和問題,選出最恰當的答案。）（6分）

(   ) 13.   (A)3:30.   (B)3:40.
          (C)3:50.   (D)4:00.
(   ) 14.   (A)Snow.   (B)Skating.
          (C)Coldness.   (D)Warm clothes.
(   ) 15.   (A)80 yuan.   (B)100 yuan.
          (C)60 yuan.   (D)120 yuan.
(   ) 16.   (A)A shop assistant.   (B)A book seller.
          (C)A librarian.   (D)A secretary.
(   ) 17.   (A)Rainy.   (B)Stormy.
          (C)Foggy.   (D)Sunny.
(   ) 18.   (A)To eat mooncakes.   (B)To set off firecrackers.
          (C)To receive red packets.   (D)To visit relatives.

Ⅳ、Listen to the dialogue and decide whether the following statements are True (T) or
    False (F). （判斷下列句子內容是否符合你所聽到的對話內容,符合的用"T"表示,不符合的
    用"F"表示。）（6分）

(   ) 19.   There are more than thirty million kinds of plants in the world.
(   ) 20.   People like decorating rooms with flowers and other plants.
(   ) 21.   People and animals only get food from plants.
(   ) 22.   Unlike animals, people can't live without plants.
(   ) 23.   People can make clothes out of cotton.
(   ) 24.   All medicines are made from plants.

25. Sports help to keep people healthy and make them live _____.

26. Sports change with the _____.

27. Sailing is _____ in warm weather.

28. _____ is good in winter.

29. People from different _____ may not be able to understand each other, but after a game on the sports field, they often become good friends.

30. One learns to fight hard, to win without pride and to _____ with grace.

全新國中會考英語聽力精選(下)
Unit 15

I、Listen and choose the right picture. (根據你所聽到的內容，選出相應的圖片。) (6分)

A.　　　　　　B.　　　　　　C.

D.　　　　　E.　　　　　F.　　　　　G.

1. _____　　　2. _____　　　3. _____

4. _____　　　5. _____　　　6. _____

II、Listen to the dialogue and choose the best answer to the question you hear. (根據你所聽到的對話和問題，選出最恰當的答案。) (10分)

(　) 7. (A)7.45.　　　　　(B)8.20.　　　　　(C)8.15.　　　　　(D)8.25.

(　) 8. (A)56940213.　　(B)56942310.　　(C)56639304.　　(D)56693304.

(　) 9. (A)At the reception desk.　　　　　(B)In Room 5018.
　　　　(C)In a restaurant.　　　　　　　(D)In a bookshop.

(　) 10. (A)By train.　　(B)By bus.　　(C)By underground. (D)By taxi.

(　) 11. (A)Go to the cinema.　　　　　(B)Have a big meal.
　　　　(C)Stay at home.　　　　　　(D)Go to the airport.

(　) 12. (A)At a restaurant.　　　　　(B)In a hotel.
　　　　(C)In a supermarket.　　　　(D)At the cinema.

(　) 13. (A)A dentist.　　(B)A doctor.　　(C)A teacher.　　(D)A trainer.

(　) 14. (A)12 years old.　(B)14 years old.　(C)15 years old.　(D)16 years old.

(　) 15. (A)Friendlier.　　　　　　　　(B)Not friendly.

(C)Not as friendly as hers.   (D)As friendly as hers.

(   ) 16. (A)He got up late this morning.

(B)He hurried off to catch a plane.

(C)He was afraid that he would be late for the train.

(D)He hurried off to catch a train.

Ⅲ、Listen to the passage and decide whether the following statements are True (T) or False (F). （判斷下列句子是否符合你所聽到的短文內容，符合的用 T 表示，不符合的用 F 表示。）（7分）

(   ) 17. According to the passage, the listeners might be the people in the city.

(   ) 18. In this country, if you are under 18 years of age, you may not buy wine, but your friend can buy it for you.

(   ) 19. The speaker told the listeners not to make unnecessary noise at night. But they can in the day time.

(   ) 20. It's important for the listeners to cross the streets by using the pedestrian crossings in England.

(   ) 21. You may buy cigarettes if you are above 16 years of age.

(   ) 22. It is against the law to put the litter in your pocket and take it home.

(   ) 23. A policeman probably makes the speech.

Ⅳ、Listen to the dialogue and fill in the blanks. （根據你聽到的對話，完成下列內容，每空格限填一詞。）（7分）

Some facts about blind and deaf people

For blind people

good __24__ skills are useful for them

they __25__ hear better than other people

they use their hearing __26__ than people with 27

For deaf people

they do things more __28__ than blind people

they never get the __29__ to hear the language

they use __30__ language to communicate

     24. _____   25. _____   26. _____   27. _____

     28. _____   29. _____   30. _____

Unit 1

> I、Listen and choose the right picture.（根據你所聽到的內容,選出相應的圖片。）（6分）

1. My pen-friend works as a postman and he is hardworking.
    （我的筆友的工作是郵差且他努力工作。）
    答案：(E)

2. Mrs. Wang is not only our Math teacher, but our good friend as well.
    （王太太不只是我們的數學老師,而且也是我們的好朋友。）
    答案：(D)

3. The Teddy Bear is my only friend and I always read books with him.
    （這泰迪熊是我唯一的朋友,我總是和他一起讀書。）
    答案：(A)

4. My father likes to play basketball with me and he looks like my close friend.
    （我父親喜歡和我一起打籃球,他看起來像我親密的朋友。）
    答案：(G)

5. Jason is not my real friend as he cares only for money.
    （傑森不是我真正的朋友因為他只在乎錢。）
    答案：(B)

6. Martin is Kitty's brother and is friendly to his little sister.
    （馬丁是凱悌的哥哥且對他的妹妹很友善。）
    答案：(F)

7. M: Who wrote this letter to you, Alice?（男：這封信是誰寫給妳的，愛麗絲？）

   W: My pen-pal Mike. He is now like my big brother.（女：我的筆友麥克。他現在就好像我哥哥一樣。）

   Q: Who is Mike?（問題：麥克是誰？）

   (A)Alice's cousin.（愛麗絲的表哥。）　　　(B)Alice's brother.（愛麗絲的哥哥。）

   (C)Alice's sister.（愛麗絲的姊姊。）　　　(D)Alice's pen-friend.（愛麗絲的筆友。）

   答案：(D)

8. M: Lisa, is your pen friend from Japan?（男：莉莎，妳的筆友是來自日本嗎？）

   W: She stayed in Japan for just several weeks. Now she lives in China. But she is Korean.（女：她只在日本待了幾個星期。現在她住在中國。但她是韓國人。）

   Q: What is Lisa's pen friend's nationality?（問題：莉莎的筆友是何國籍？）

   (A)German.（德國。）　(B)Japanese.（日本。）

   (C)Korean.（韓國。）　(D)Chinese.（中國。）

   答案：(C)

9. M: I want to borrow this book. It tells us how to write letters.

   　　（男：我想借這本書。它告訴我們如何寫信。）

   W: So you often write letters?（女：所以你經常寫信嗎？）

   M: Yes, I have many pen-friends.（男：是的，我有很多筆友。）

   Q: Where does this dialogue take place?（問題：這段會話在哪裡發生？）

   (A)In a bookstore.（在一間書店。）　　　(B)In a library.（在一間圖書館。）

   (C)In a hospital.（在一所醫院。）　　　(D)In a cinema.（在一間電影院。）

   答案：(B)

10. M: Daisy, what is the most important thing for us to remember when we make friends?（男：黛西，我們在交朋友的時候需要記住最重要的是什麼？）

    W: I think to be honest is quite essential. Do you think so?

    　　（女：我認為誠實是頗重要的。你也這樣想嗎？）

    M: Yes, I agree. And in my opinion, to be kind and helpful is also important.

    　　（男：是的，我同意。而且在我看來，親切和樂於助人也很重要。）

    Q: What are they talking about?（問題：他們在聊什麼？）

    (A)When we need to make friends.（我們何時需要交朋友。）

    (B)Why we need to make friends.（我們為何需要交朋友。）

    (C)When to make friends.（交朋友的時機。）

    (D)How to make friends.（如何交朋友。）

    答案：(D)

11. M: It is raining outside. Will you still go to the market to shop with your friends?（男：外面正下著雨。你仍然會跟妳朋友們去市場購物嗎？）

W: I'm afraid I will be all wet. So I decide to go shopping tomorrow.
（女：我恐怕會濕透透。所以我決定明天去購物。）

M: What a coincidence! There will be special prices on Tuesday. You are so lucky.（男：多麼巧啊！星期二將會有特價。妳真幸運。）

Q: What day is it today?（問題：今天星期幾？）

(A)Monday.（星期一。）   (B)Sunday.（星期日。）

(C)Tuesday.（星期二。）   (D)Wednesday.（星期三。）

答案：(A)

12. M: As we are friends, may I have your e-mail address?
（男：既然我們是朋友，我可以跟妳要電郵地址嗎？）

W: OK. It's L-L-O-O-V-V-E-E @ hotmail.com.
（女：好啊。L-L-O-O-V-V-E-E 小老鼠 hotmail.com.）

M: Let's keep in touch.（男：讓我們保持聯絡。）

Q: How will they keep in touch?（問題：他們將如何保持聯絡？）

(A)By visiting their houses.（去彼此家拜訪。）

(B)By writing ordinary mails.（寫普通信件。）

(C)By writing e-mails.（寫電子郵件。）

(D)By phone.（用電話。）

答案：(C)

13. M: Excuse me, how can I get to the People's Park?
（男：不好意思，我要如何去大眾公園？）

W: I suggest you walk to the nearest underground station. Then you will easily know how to get there.
（女：我建議你走到最靠近的地鐵站。然後你將很容易得知如何去那裡。）

M: So, I have to turn left or right?（男：所以，我該轉左邊還是右邊？）

W: Just walk straight. You will find one within 5 minutes.
（女：就直走。你將在五分鐘以內找到一個。）

Q: How will the man go to the nearest station?
（問題：這位男士將如何去最靠近的車站？）

(A)By underground.（搭地鐵。）   (B)By taxi.（搭計程車。）

(C)By bus.（搭巴士。）   (D)On foot.（走路。）

答案：(D)

14. M: Do you often watch cartoons?（男：妳常常看卡通嗎？）

W: Cartoons are not my favorite and I only enjoy action movies.
（女：卡通不是我的最愛，我只愛看動作片。）

M: I like to watch horror movies and adventure ones.

（男：我喜歡看恐怖片和冒險片。）

Q: What are the lady's favorite movies?（問題：這位淑女最愛哪種電影？）

(A)Cartoons.（卡通。）   (B)Action movies.（動作片。）

(C)Horror movies.（恐怖片。）   (D)Adventure movies.（冒險片。）

答案：(B)

15. M: How many friends do you have?（男：妳有多少位朋友？）

W: I have so many friends around me.（女：我有那麼多朋友在我身邊。）

M: It just means you don't have real friends.

（男：這只表示妳沒有真正的朋友。）

Q: What does the man mean?（問題：這位男士的意思是？）

(A)It's impossible to make real friends with so many people.

（和那麼多人成為真正的朋友是不可能的。）

(B)In fact, the woman has no friends around her.

（事實上，這位女士沒有朋友在她身邊。）

(C)The woman is telling a lie and she is dishonest.（這位女士說謊，她不誠實。）

(D)The man wants to tell the woman not to make many friends.

（這位男士想要告訴這位女士不要交很多朋友。）

答案：(A)

16. W: Mike, when will the film begin?（女：麥克，電影何時將會開始？）

M: Let me check the ticket. It will begin at 8.

（男：讓我查看電影票。它將在八點開始。）

W: Can we meet at the entrance at 7:55?

（女：我們可以七點五十五分在入口見面嗎？）

M: Why not ten minutes earlier? We can buy some snacks there.

（男：為何不提早十分鐘？我們可以在那裡買些點心。）

W: Good idea! See you soon.（女：好主意！待會見。）

Q: When will they meet at the entrance?（問題：他們將幾點在入口見面？）

(A)At 8.（八點整）   (B)At 7:45.（七點四十五分）

(C)At 7:55.（七點五十五分）   (D)At 8:05.（八點五分）

答案：(B)

Ⅲ、Listen to the passage and tell whether the following statements are true or false.

（判斷下列句子是否符合你聽到的短文內容,符合用 T 表示,不符合用 F 表示）（7分）

    As a human being, one can hardly do without a friend, for life without friends will be a lonely journey in the dark sea or one in the desert. Truly, a friend gives out light and warmth like a lamp. For this reason, I have always felt it a lucky time if a friend comes to me in my sadness, cheer me up in my low spirits, or share my happiness with me. It is wonderful, too, to feel that someone is standing by me and ready to provide help and encouragement during my growth.

　　身為人類，一個人幾乎不能沒有朋友，因為沒有朋友的人生將會是在黑暗的海洋上或是沙漠中一個孤單的旅程。真的，一位朋友帶來如同一盞燈的光和溫暖。因此，如果一個朋友在我悲傷時來看我，在我心情沮喪時來鼓勵我，或者和我分享我的快樂，我總是感到那是幸運的時光。在我的成長中感受到某人站在我身邊準備好提供幫助和鼓勵，也是很棒的。

A real friend is considered even more precious than a priceless pearl or an expensive house. The old saying "A friend in need is a friend indeed" has told us what true friends mean.

　　一個真正的朋友被視為比一顆無價的珍珠或一幢昂貴的房子還要珍貴。一句古老諺語「患難見真情」告訴我們真朋友的意義。

Still, it is natural that different people have different ideas in making friends. Some think it important to make friends with whom they may share the same interests or hobbies with. Others are going to find friends so as to get some favors or special help. And I am one of those who think very little of similarity or position or power. As long as a person is warm-hearted, selfless, honest, open-minded, but not cruel, cold, shortsighted nor narrow-minded, I am willing to make friends with him or her, give my support and help, and remain unchanged to him or her all my life.

　　然而，自然地，不同的人對交朋友有不同的想法。有些人認為和可以分享共同興趣或嗜好的人交朋友是重要的。其他人則尋找些可以得到益處或特別幫助的朋友。而我是那些對身分或地位或權力想得很少的人當中的一個。只要這個人有溫暖的心、無私、誠實、思想開放，但不無情、冷漠、短視或思想狹隘，我就很願意和他或她交朋友，提供我的支持和幫助，且一輩子對他或她維持不變。

17. Human beings can't do without friends. （人類不能沒朋友。）

　　答案：(T 對)

18. The writer doesn't want her friends to come to her when she is very sad.

　　（筆者不想要她的朋友在她悲傷時來看她。）

　　答案：(F 錯)

19. According to the writer, a real friend is the same as a precious pearl.

　　（根據筆者，一個真正的朋友就像一顆珍貴的珍珠。）

　　答案：(F 錯)

20. To have the same hobbies or interests is the first thing that people consider when they make friends.

　　（擁有相同的嗜好或興趣是人們交朋友時首先考慮的。）

　　答案：(F 錯)

21. The writer wants to make friends with those who have enough power.

（筆者想要和有足夠權力的人們交朋友。）

答案：(F 錯)

22. The writer doesn't want to make friends with people who wear glasses.

（筆者不想要和戴眼鏡的人們交朋友。）

答案：(F 錯)

23. The support the writer gives to her friend will never change all her life.

（筆者對她朋友提供的支持將一輩子都不改變。）

答案：(T 對)

IV、Listen to the passage and fill in the blanks with proper words.（聽短文,用最恰當的填空,每格限填一詞）（共 7 分）

I have a pen-pal called John from the United States. He is a middle school student of Grade 2. He is good at math and physics. Of course, he is a top student in his class. When I started to write to him, he invited me to teach him Chinese. It seems that he has lots of interests and he plans to learn everything strange to him. In his letter, he tells me many stories in his country, his school and his family as well. Anyway, he is a good boy. I love him and like to make friends with him. I hope that he will come to China some day in the future. Then, we can communicate with each other and have a good time together.

我有位筆友叫約翰，來自美國。他是一名中學二年級的學生。他在數學和物理方面很拿手。當然，他在他的班上名列前茅。當我開始寫信給他，他請我教他中文。他似乎有很多興趣並且計畫學習任何對他來說新奇的東西。在他的信中，他告訴我很多他的國家、他的學校還有他的家庭的故事。不管怎麼說，他是個好孩子。我愛他並且想和他做朋友。我希望他未來有一天會來到中國。那時，我們可以互相溝通並一起玩樂。

- The nationality of the pen-friend is __24__.

  （該筆友的國籍是美國。）

- Now he studies in Grade __25__ in a Junior High School.

  （目前他就讀國中的二年級。）

- The subjects he does well in are __26__ and math.

  （他拿手的科目是物理和數學。）

- The pen-friend __27__ me to teach him Chinese at the beginning.

  （該筆友最初請我教他中文。）

- He seems to have lots of __28__.

  （他似乎有很多興趣。）

- In his letters, he shares with me many __29__ in his country.

  （在他的信中，他和我分享很多他國家的故事。）

- I hope to meet him in China so that we can __30__ with each other better.

  （我希望和他在中國見面這樣我們可以彼此溝通得更好。）

24. 答案：American
25. 答案：Two／2
26. 答案：physics
27. 答案：invited
28. 答案：interests
29. 答案：stories
30. 答案：communicate

Unit 2

> I、Listen and choose the right picture.（根據你所聽到的內容，選出相應的圖片。）（6分）

A.　　　　　　　　B.　　　　　　　　C.

D.　　　　　　　　E.　　　　　　　　F.　　　　　　　　G.

1. Have you ever watched lion dances? It's quite popular in the Chinatown in Melbourne.
   (你看過舞獅嗎？它在墨爾本的中國城相當受到歡迎。)
   答案：(E)

2. It shines brightly today. Shall we go to the park for a walk?
   (今天天氣晴朗。我們去公園散步好嗎？)
   答案：(B)

3. Don't forget to wash your hands before eating. (吃東西前別忘了洗手。)
   答案：(D)

4. Jimmy, cheers! We haven't met for a long time. (Jimmy，乾杯。我們好久沒見面了。)
   答案：(F)

5. Do you enjoy making snowmen in winter? (冬天的時候你喜歡做雪人嗎？)
   答案：(G)

6. Take a hot shower and you will feel much better. (沖個熱水澡，你就會覺得好一點。)
   答案：(C)

7. W: Why hasn't Linda come? It's nearly 3.30.(W: Linda 為什麼還不來？已經要三點半了。)

   M: I told her to be here at 3.15. She has been late for fifteen minutes.

   (M: 我告訴她三點十五分來這兒。她已經遲到十五分鐘了。)

   Question: What time did the man ask Linda to come? (問題：那男人要 Linda 幾點來？)

   (A)Before 3.15.(三點十五分以前。)　　　　(B)At 3.30.(三點三十分。)

   (C)At 3.15.(三點十五分。)　　　　　　　(D)At 3.50.(三點五十分。)

   答案：(C)

8. W: Hi, Tom, I am afraid I have to get my book back. Can you return it to me?

   (W: Tom，我恐怕得要把我的書拿回來。你明天能還我嗎？)

   M: Oh, sorry! It isn't with me. I left it at the doctor's.

   (M: 喔，對不起。它不在我這裡。我把它放在醫生家了。)

   Question: Whose book do you think it is? (問題：你認為這是誰的書？)

   (A)The girl's.(女孩的。)　　　　　　　(B)The boy's.(男孩的。)

   (C)The doctor's.(醫生的。)　　　　　　(D)Someone else's.(某個人的。)

   答案：(A)

9. W: Danny, what about your examination?(W: Danny，你考試考得怎樣？)

   M: I achieved B grades in Chinese and physics.(M: 我的中文和物理都拿了 B。)

   W: Not bad! And I'm sure you are good at English and music.

   (W: 還不差啊！我相信你的英文和音樂考得很好。)

   M: Yes, they are my favourite subjects. But I failed in history. I just can't remember all the years and events!(M: 是的，它們是我最喜歡的科目。但是我歷史當掉了。我就是記不得那些年分和事件。)

   W: Poor boy!(W: 可憐的孩子！)

   Question: Which subjects are Danny's favorite? (問題：Danny 最喜歡哪些科目？)

   (A)Chinese and physics.(中文和物理。)　　(B)English and music.(英文和音樂。)

   (C)History and music.(歷史和音樂。)　　　(D)English and history.(英文和歷史。)

   答案：(B)

10. M: Hello, May. We are sure coming to see you next week.

    (M: 哈囉，May。我們下星期一定會來看你。)

    W: I'm glad to hear it. Have you got your plane tickets yet?

    (W: 我很高興聽到你們要來。你買機票了嗎？)

    M: I've already got mine, but Judy hasn't got hers yet. (M: 我已經買了票，但是 Judy 還沒買。)

    W: Why is that?(W: 為什麼？)

    M: She hasn't saved enough money. She is coming to see you by train next week.

(M: 她存的錢不夠。她下星期會搭火車來看你。)

Question: How will Judy go to see her friend next week?

(問題：Judy 下星期要怎麼去看她朋友？)

(A)By plane.(搭飛機。)　　　　　　　(B)By car. (搭車。)

(C)By train. (搭火車。)　　　　　　　(D)By ship. (搭船。)

答案：(C)

11. W: My mother is a manager. She's always busy. What does your mother do, Peter?
    (W: 我母親是一位經理。她總是很忙。Peter，你母親做甚麼？)

    M: She's an airhostess for Air France. But when she was a teenager, she hoped to be a pilot. She enjoys her job. (M: 她是法國航空的空中小姐。但是在她還是個青少年的時候，她希望當飛行員。)

    Question: What job does Peter's mother do? (問題：Peter 的母親做甚麼工作？)

    (A)A manager.(經理。)　　　　　　(B)A businesswoman.(女企業家。)

    (C)A pilot.(飛行員。)　　　　　　(D)An airhostess.(空中小姐。)

    答案：(D)

12. W: I have been to France. I flew back a week ago.(W: 我去了法國。我一個星期前飛回來的。)

    M: Did you meet Mary and Joan? They've gone to Paris on business.
    (M: 你見到 Mary 和 Joan 嗎？她們去巴黎出差了。)

    W: Yes, I happened to meet them. When I came back, they had already stayed there for two weeks. (W: 是，我碰巧遇見她們。當我回來的時候，她們已經在那兒待了兩個星期。)

    M: Are they coming back soon?(M: 她們很快就會回來嗎？)

    W: Yes, they said they would return after a week.(W: 是，她們說她們一個星期後回來。)

    Question: How long have Mary and Joan been in France?

    (問題：Mary 和 Joan 在法國待了多久？)

    (A)About two weeks.(大約兩個星期。)　　(B)About three weeks.(大約三個星期。)

    (C)About four weeks.(大約四個星期。)　　(D)About five weeks.(大約五個星期。)

    答案：(B)

13. W: I've got two tickets for the film American Pie.(W: 我有兩張「美國派」的電影票。)

    M: May I have one?(M: 可以給我一張嗎？)

    W: Certainly. I think it's time to leave.(W: 當然可以。我想是時候出發了。)

    M: Isn't it still early?(M: 現在不是還早嗎？)

    W: Look! It's twenty to two now. It will begin in fifteen minutes.
    (W: 看！現在是一點四十分。它十五分鐘後開演。)

    M: You're right, let's hurry.(M: 沒錯，我們得快一點。)

    Question: What time will the film begin? (問題：電影幾點開始？)

    (A)At 2.55. (兩點五十五分。)　　　　(B)At 1.55. (一點五十五分。)

    (C)At 2.40. (兩點四十分。)　　　　(D)At 1.40.(一點四十分。)

    答案：(B)

14. M: What can I do for you?(M: 我能為你效勞嗎？)

W: I'd like to have a look at the thick book.(W: 我要看一看那本厚厚的書。)

M: Which one?(M: 哪一本？)

W: The big red one on the shelf.(W: 書架上很大的、紅色的那本。)

M: Here you are. It's expensive. It costs ten pounds.(M: 給你。這本書很貴。要十英鎊。)

Question: Where are they probably talking? (問題：他們可能在哪裡談話？)

(A)In a library.(圖書館。)　　　　　　(B)In a book shop.(書店。)

(C)In a reading room. (閱覽室。)　　　(D)In the man's home.(那男人的家。)

答案：(B)

15. M: It's too far away to go on foot. I think you should ride a bike.

(M:走路太遠了。我認為你該騎腳踏車。)

W: It's convenient to go by bike, but the traffic is often heavy.

(W: 騎腳踏車很方便，但是交通常常很擁擠。)

M: Then what about taking a bus?(M: 那麼搭公車如何？)

W: But waiting for a bus takes a lot of time. I'd like to take an underground.

(W: 但是等公車要花好久的時間。我想搭地鐵。)

M: That's good.(M: 那很好。)

Question: How would the woman go?(問題：那女人怎麼去？)

(A)By bus.(搭公車。)　　　　　(B)By bike.(騎腳踏車。)

(C)By underground. (搭地鐵。)　　(D)By train.(搭火車。)

答案：(C)

16. M: Can you spell the word "government"?(M: 你能拼出「government」這個單字嗎？)

W: Yes, g-o-v-e-r-m-e-n-t.(W: 可以，g-o-v-e-r-m-e-n-t。)

M: No, you are wrong. You miss an "n".(M: 不，你錯了。你少了一個「n」。)

W: Oh, I see.(W: 喔，我知道了。)

Question: Could the boy spell the word "government"?

(那男孩能拼出「government」這個單字嗎？)

(A)No, he can't.(不，他不能。)

(B)Yes, he can.(是，他可以。)

(C)No, he couldn't. (不，他不可能。)

(D)Yes, he could. (是的，他可能。)

答案：(D)

Ⅲ、Listen to the passage and decide whether the following statements are True (T) or False (F). (判斷下列句子是否符合你所聽到的短文內容，符合的用 T 表示，不符合的用 F 表示。)（7分）

Dear Angela,

Thanks for your letter. Now I want to tell you about the four seasons in Canberra.

Spring in Canberra lasts for three months, from September to November. I love the spring here. The trees in the street have lots of small white flowers and the weather is nice. At the beginning of spring, it is cool and sometimes rains. At the end of spring, the weather is warm.

It is often dry and very hot in the middle of summer. Sometimes we have four or five days at 45 °C! Our summer holiday starts at the beginning of December and ends at the beginning of February. I go swimming every day. We usually go to the sea for a week in January. It is windy there and the sea is very cool.

In autumn, the trees are all orange and brown. Our autumn is March, April and May.

In winter, it snows in some places. We go skiing in the Snowy Mountains every winter in June, July or August. Sometimes it is rainy but it is usually very cold. Often the sky is very blue, and you never see any clouds. It is my favourite season. What is your favourite season?

Write soon.

Love,
Judy

親愛的 Angela，

謝謝你的來信。我現在想告訴你有關 Canberra 的四季。

Canberra 的春天從九月到十一月共持續三個月。我很愛這裡的春天。街道上的樹木有好多白色的小花，天氣也很棒。春天剛開始的時候，天氣很冷而且常常下雨。春天快結束的時候，天氣就很溫暖。

夏天的中期通常非常乾熱。我們有時候有四、五天是攝氏四十五度！我們的暑假在十二月初開始，然後在二月初結束。我每天去游泳。一月的時候我們常常去海邊一個星期。那兒有風，海非常清涼。

秋天的時候，樹木都是橘色和棕色的。我們的秋天是三月、四月和五月。

冬天的時候，某些地方會下雪。每到冬天的六、七、八月，我們常去雪山滑雪。有時會下雨，但是天氣非常冷。天空非常的藍，你完全看不到雲。這是我最喜歡的季節。你最喜歡的季節是甚麼呢？

快回信。

愛你的
Judy

17. Angela has got a penfriend in Australia.(Angela 有一個澳洲的筆友。)

答案：(T 對)

18. Spring in Canberra lasts for about four months. (Canberra 的春天大約持續四個月。)

答案：(F 錯)

19. Summer in Canberra usually starts at the beginning of February. (Canberra 的夏天通常在二月初開始。)

答案：(F 錯)

20. Judy enjoys going to the sea in summer. (Judy 喜歡在夏天去海邊。)

答案：(T 對)

21. Judy doesn't talk much about autumn in Canberra in her letter. (Judy 在她的信中並沒有談到很多關於 Canberra 秋天的事。)

答案：(T 對)

22. Winter in Canberra is always rainy and cold. (Canberra 的冬天總是下雨而且寒冷。)

答案：(F 錯)

23. Judy's favourite season is spring.(Judy 最喜歡的季節是春天。)

答案：(F 錯)

IV、Listen to the passage and fill in the blanks. （根據你聽到的短文，完成下列內容，每空格限填一詞。）（7 分）

Anita studies at a middle school in Guangzhou. Every day, she wakes up at six o'clock in the morning. She quickly brushes her teeth and washes her face. Then she reads English for half an hour. She has breakfast at seven o'clock. She usually has two pieces of bread and a glass of milk.

Anita 在廣州念中學。她每天早上六點醒來。她很快地刷牙洗臉。然後她念半個小時的英文。她七點吃早餐。她常吃兩片麵包和一杯牛奶。

After breakfast, Anita goes to school. She lives near school and always walks there. She usually gets to school at eight o'clock, and usually has six lessons. Anita loves English very much, and always gets an A。She usually gets a B in her other subjects.

Anita 吃完早餐後去上學。她住得離學校很近，所以總是走路去。她通常在八點到校，然後有六堂課。Anita 非常愛英文，而且一直拿 A。她通常在其他的科目上拿 B。

After school, Anita usually walks home at four o'clock in the afternoon. Her favourite sport is table tennis. She plays table tennis with her classmates at school once a week.

放學後，Anita 通常在下午四點走路回家。她最喜歡的運動是桌球。她每一星期一次和她的同學在學校打桌球。

Anita often has an early dinner. She begins to do her homework at six o'clock and completes it in one or two hours. She usually goes to bed at nine o'clock.

Anita 晚飯常吃得很早。她六點開始寫功課，在一到兩個小時之內寫完。她通常九點睡覺。

- Anita __24__ up at 6 a.m. (Anita 早上六點_____。)
- After doing some washing, she __25__ English for half an hour. (做了一些清洗之後，她___半個小時的英文。)
- At __26__, she has breakfast. (她___點吃早餐。)
- At 8 a.m., she __27__ to school. (她早上八點_____學校。)
- At 4 p.m., she __28__ home. (她下午四點_____回家。)
- At __29__, she begins to do her homework. (她_____點開始寫功課。)
- At 9 p.m., she goes to __30__. (她晚上九點_____。)

24. 答案：wakes (清醒。)
25. 答案：reads (閱讀)
26. 答案：7 a.m. (早上七點)
27. 答案：gets (到達)
28. 答案：walks (走路)
29. 答案：6 p.m. (下午六點)
30. 答案：bed (床)

Unit 3

I 、Listen and choose the right picture.

A.   B.   C.

D.   E.   F.   G.

1. Please open the window a bit. We need some fresh air inside.
    (請把窗戶打開一點。我們需要一些新鮮空氣在室內。)
    答案：(G)

2. What a funny man! His pet is a ... P-I-G, pig!
    (多有趣的一個人！他的寵物是一隻…ㄓㄨ，豬！)
    答案：(E)

3. It's very cold outside. You ought to put on your overcoat!
    (外面很冷。你應該穿上你的大衣。)
    答案：(A)

4. Swing, swing, swing! High in the sky! Waving and shaking! It's fun! Win, win, win!
    (盪啊，盪啊，盪啊！高高在天空！揮舞著搖晃著！好好玩！勝利，勝利，勝利！)
    答案：(C)

5. Rope and hope! Jumping and shaking! It's your turn! Let's go on!
    (繩子和希望！跳躍著搖晃著！輪到你了！讓我們繼續！)
    答案：(D)

6. Stop doing that! It's dangerous to ride so fast down the mountain!
(不要那樣做！下山騎那麼快很危險！)
答案：(B)

Ⅱ、Listen to the dialogue and choose the best answer to the question you hear.

7. M: Excuse me, where is the nearest supermarket? (男：不好意思，最近的超市在哪裡？)
W: I'm sorry. I am new here too. (女：抱歉。我對這一帶也不熟。)
M: Could you tell me where the No. 48 bus is? (男：您可以告訴我四十八路巴士在哪裡嗎？)
W: At the end of the street. (女：在這條街底。)
M: Thank you very much. (男：多謝您。)
Question: Where is the nearest supermarket? (問題：最靠近的超市在哪裡？)
(A)At the corner of the street. (街上的轉角處) (B)At the end of the street. (街道底)
(C)At the No. 48 bus stop. (48 路公車站)　　　 (D)The lady has no idea. (這位女士不知道。)
答案：(D)

8. M: What can I do for you, madam? (男：有什麼我能為您效勞的，夫人？)
W: I want to buy a handbag. (女：我想買個手提包。)
M: Do you like the blue one or the brown one? (男：您喜歡藍色那個或是咖啡色那個？)
W: I like brown better than blue. How much is it?
　　 (女：和藍色的比起來我比較喜歡咖啡色的。它多少錢？)
M: 30 dollars, please. (男：三十美金，麻煩您。)
Question: What is the woman going to buy? (問題：這位女士要買什麼？)
(A)A blue handbag. (一個藍色手提包)　　　 (B)A brown handbag. (一個咖啡色手提包)
(C)13 dollars. (13 元)　　　　　　　　　　 (D)30 dollars. (30 元)
答案：(B)

9. M: Linda, show me your school report, please. (男：琳達，請給我看妳的學校報告。)
W: Here you are, Daddy. (女：在這裡，爸。)
M: You got good marks for English and chemistry, but you didn't do well enough in maths.
　　 (男：妳在英文和化學成績很好，但是妳在數學上表現不夠好。)
W: I'm sorry, Daddy. I'll work harder next time. (女：抱歉，爸。我下次會更用功。)
Question: What subject is Linda poor in? (問題：琳達弱的科目是什麼？)
(A)Physics. (物理)　　 (B)English. (英文)　　 (C)Maths. (數學)　　 (D)Chemistry. (化學)
答案：(C)

10. W: Excuse me, where is the No.49 bus stop? (女：不好意思，四十九路巴士的站在哪裡？)
M: It's just on the other side of the street, near the post office.
　　 (男：它就在街道的另一側，靠近郵局。)
W: Thank you. (女：謝謝。)
M: You are welcome. (男：不客氣。)

Question: What is the lady looking for? (問題：這位女士正在找什麼？)

(A)A No. 49 bus. (49 路巴士)　　　　(B)The bus stop. (巴士站)

(C)The post office. (郵局)　　　　(D)A street. (一條街)

答案：(B)

11. W: May I speak to Mr. John Gray? (女：我可以和約翰蓋瑞先生講話嗎？)

M: Speaking, who's that calling? (男：我就是，您哪裡找？)

W: It's Ellen. Ellen Smith. (女：我是艾倫。艾倫史密斯。)

Question: Who are on the phone? (問題：在電話上的是誰？)

(A)John and Ellen. (約翰和艾倫)

(B)Miss Gray and Mrs. Smith. (蓋瑞小姐和史密斯太太)

(C)Mr. Smith and Miss Gray. (史密斯先生和蓋瑞小姐)

(D)John and Gray. (約翰和蓋瑞)

答案：(A)

12. W: Yesterday I went to see a new film. What about you?

(女：昨天我去看了一場電影。那你呢？)

M: I visited the photo show instead of seeing a film.

(男：我參觀了一個攝影展而沒有去看電影。)

Question: What did the man do yesterday? (問題：這位男士昨天做了什麼？)

(A)He watched TV at home. (他在家看電視。)

(B)He went to see a film. (他去看電影。)

(C)He visited the photo show. (他參觀了一個攝影展。)

(D)He visited the flower show. (他參觀了花展。)

答案：(C)

13. M: I can't find my pen. It was here on the desk this morning. Have you seen it, Jim?

(男：我找不到我的筆。它早上在這邊的書桌上。妳有看到它嗎，金？)

W: Yes, I wrote a letter with it and then I put it in the desk drawer.

(女：有，我用它寫了一封信然後我把它放在書桌抽屜裡。)

Question: What did the girl do with the pen? (問題：這位女孩把那支筆怎麼了？)

(A)She gave it to Jim. (她把它給了 Jim。)

(B)She put it on the desk. (她把它放在桌子上。)

(C)She put it in the desk drawer (她把它放在書桌抽屜裡。)

(D)She didn't see it. (她沒看到筆。)

答案：(C)

14. W: It's nearly 12 o'clock. I'm hungry. Look, there's a KFC restaurant over there.

(女：將近十二點了。我餓了。你看，在那邊有個肯德基餐廳。)

M: But it's expensive, isn't it? (男：但它頗貴，不是嗎？)

W: No, it isn't and the chicken there is nice. (女：不會，它不貴而且那邊的雞肉很好。)

M: OK. Let's go then. (男：好吧。那我們就去。)

Question: Why are they talking about the KFC fast food?

(問題：他們為什麼在談論肯德基速食？)

(A)Because the restaurant is new. (因為該餐廳是新的。)

(B)Because they enjoy fast food. (因為他們喜歡速食。)

(C)Because the food there is not expensive. (因為那裏的食物不貴。)

(D)Because they are hungry and want to have lunch there.

　　(因為他們餓了且想要在那邊吃午餐。)

答案：(D)

15. W: Why are you in such a hurry, Mr Black?

　　(女：你為何如此匆忙，布萊克先生？)

M: I'll leave for Beijing to attend an important meeting. The train will start off in less than two hours. ((男：我將出發去北京出席一個重要的會議。火車將在不到兩小時以內開車。)

W: So you must get everything ready before three o'clock.

　　(女：所以你必須在三點以前把一切準備好。)

Question: How will Mr Black go to Beijing? (問題：布萊克先生將怎麼去北京？)

(A)By train. (搭火車)　　　　　　　　　(B)By plane. (搭飛機)

(C)In about two hours. (在大約兩小時後)　　(D)Before three o'clock. (在三點前)

答案：(A)

16. M: Lily, I haven't seen you for nearly a month. Where have you been these days?

　　(男：莉莉，我快要一個月沒看到妳了。這些日子妳都在哪裡？)

W: I went to Australia with my husband for my holiday.

　　(女：我和我先生去了澳洲度假。)

M: Did you have a good time there? (男：你們在那邊玩得開心嗎？)

W: Yes. And I'm going to France next summer holiday.

　　(女：是啊。而且我下個暑假要去法國。)

M: What a coincidence! Me too. (男：多巧啊！我也是。)

Question: Where did Lily go during the holiday? (問題：莉莉在假期中去了哪裡？)

(A)America. (美國)　　(B)Australia. (澳洲)　　(C)France. (法國)　　(D)Japan. (日本)

答案：(B)

Ⅲ、Listen to the passage and decide whether the following statements are True (T) or False (F).

There will be a lecture at the school lecture hall on Wednesday evening. It's about how to protect eyesight. Nancy has got two tickets, one for herself and the other for her classmate, Henry. Henry is getting quite nearsighted. The lecture is just what he needs. Nancy often forgets things. It's Tuesday today. But she tells Henry to wait for her at the gate of the lecture hall in the evening. There are only five minutes left when Nancy gets there. She shows the tickets. But the ticket-collector won't let them in. The tickets are for tomorrow. The ticket-collector is very kind. There are a couple of tickets for today left. He lets them have the tickets. But it's not the same lecture as tomorrow's. It's about how to train the memory. That's just what Nancy needs.

　　星期三晚上在學校大講堂將會有一場講座。它是關於如何保護視力。南西有兩張票，一張她自己用而另一張給她的同學，亨利。亨利近視得頗重。此講座正好是他需要的。南西常常忘記事情。今天是星期二。但是她告訴亨利晚上在大講堂的大門口等她。當南西到達那裡時只剩下五分鐘了。她把票亮出來。但是收票員不讓他們進去。這票是明天的。收票員很好心。有兩張今天的票剩下。他把票給了他們。但這和明天是不同的講座。這是關於如何訓練記憶力的。正好是南西需要的。

17. There is a lecture on Wednesday evening and another lecture on Thursday evening.
　　（星期三晚上有一場講座而星期四晚上有另一場講座。）
　　答案：(F 錯)

18. The Wednesday's lecture is about how to protect eyesight.
　　（星期三的講座是關於如何保護視力。）
　　答案：(T 對)

19. Nancy is sure that Henry will be glad to listen to the lecture.
　　（南西確定亨利將會很高興聽這場講座。）
　　答案：(T 對)

20. Nancy was late for the lecture. (那場講座南西遲到了。)
　　答案：(F 錯)

21. The ticket-collector was a very kind man. (收票員是位很好心的男士。)
　　答案：(T 對)

22. Nancy and Henry are not allowed to enter because they are late.
　　（南西和亨利不被准許入場因為他們遲到了。）
　　答案：(F 錯)

23. It seems that Nancy doesn't remember things very well. (看樣子南西記性不太好。)
　　答案：(T 對)

IV、Listen to the passage and fill in the blanks.

　　Yesterday was Eddie's birthday. He got a lot of presents from his friends and family. All the gifts were wrapped in coloured paper. Some of the packages were large, but others were very small. Some were heavy, but others were light. One square package was blue; there was a book in it. Another one was long and narrow; it had an umbrella in the pink paper. Eddie's sister gave him a big, round package. He thought it was a ball, but it wasn't. When he removed the yellow paper that covered it, he saw that it was a globe of the world. After that his brother gave Eddie another gift. It was a big box wrapped in green paper. Eddie opened it and found another box covered with red paper. He removed the paper and saw the third box — this one was blue in colour. Then he saw his brother's gift. He was very happy. It was just what Eddie wanted — a portable computer.

昨天是艾迪的生日。他收到很多來自朋友們和家人的禮物。全部的禮物都包著彩色的紙。有一些包裝很大，但其他則很小。有一些很重，但其他的輕。有一個正方形包裹是藍色的；裡面有一本書。另一個又長又窄；它是一把包著粉紅色紙的雨傘。艾迪的姊妹給他一個大的圓形包裹。他以為那是個球，但它不是。當他打開包住它的黃色紙，他看到那是個地球儀。那之後艾迪的兄弟給他另一個禮物。它是個包著綠色紙的大盒子。艾迪打開它而發現了另一個包著紅色紙的盒子。他打開包裝紙而看到第三個盒子——這一個的顏色是藍色的。然後他看到他哥哥的禮物。他很高興。那正是艾迪想要的——一台攜帶型電腦。

- Someone sent Eddie a long and __24.__ package with pink paper outside. It was an __25.__.

  (某人給了艾迪一個又長又窄外面包著粉紅色紙的包裹。它是一把傘。)

- Someone sent Eddie a square package with __26.__ paper outside and a book inside.

  (某人給了艾迪一個正方形外面有藍色紙的包裹裡面是一本書。)

- Eddie also received a globe of the world packed in a big, __27.__ package with yellow paper from his __28.__.

  (艾迪也發現了一個地球儀，包在一個大圓形黃色的包裝紙的包裹裡，來自他姊妹。)

- Eddie received a portable computer packed with __29.__ boxes in green, red and blue paper from his __30.__.

  (艾迪發現了一台攜帶型電腦以三個分別是綠色紅色和藍色的盒子裝著，來自他兄弟。)

24. 答案：narrow (窄)
25. 答案：umbrella (雨傘)
26. 答案：blue (藍色)
27. 答案：round (圓形)
28. 答案：sister (姊妹)
29. 答案：three (三個)
30. 答案：brother (兄弟)

全新國中會考英語聽力精選(下)原文及參考答案
Unit 4

I、Listen and choose the right picture.（根據你聽到的內容,選出相應的圖片。）（6分）

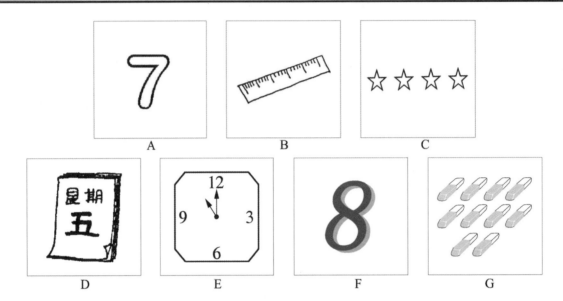

A　　　　　　　B　　　　　　　C

D　　　　　　　E　　　　　　　F　　　　　　　G

1. Eight is a lucky number in China while maybe not in other countries.
   （八在中國是個幸運數字然而在其他國家就未必。）
   答案：(F)

2. Yesterday we stayed in a four-star hotel and the service was nice.
   （昨天我們住宿在一間四星旅館，服務很好。）
   答案：(C)

3. If we add two rubbers to eight, how many on earth can we get finally?
   （如果我們將八個像皮擦加上兩個，我們到底最後會有幾個？）
   答案：(G)

4. It's eleven o'clock sharp and lunch will be ready soon.
   （現在十一點整，午餐很快就會準備好。）
   答案：(E)

5. Rulers are used to tell the length of objects.（尺是被用來測知物體的長度。）
   答案：(B)

6. We often eat out on Friday night and attend some evening clubs.
   （我們常常星期五晚上出去外面吃並去參加一些夜間俱樂部。）
   答案：(D)

7. W: How many students in your class will take part in the Physics Competition?（女：你的班上有多少位學生會去參加體能競賽？）

    M: Two fifths of the students in my class will join in the contest.

    （男：我們班五分之二的學生會加入比賽。）

    W: But what's the population of your class?（女：但是你班上人數是多少？）

    M: Twenty two girls and eighteen boys in all.

    （男：總共二十二位女孩和十八位男孩。）

    Q: How many students in the boy's class will take part in the Physics Competition?（問題：這位男孩的班上多少人會參加體能競賽。）

    (A)16.　　　　　(B)40.　　　　　(C)22.　　　　　(D)18.

    答案：(A)

8. W: When on earth does the plane take off for Paris? I miss my boyfriend.

    （女：到底飛機何時才會起飛去巴黎呢？我想念我男朋友。）

    M: The plane has been delayed for three hours. I was told that we could take off in half an hour.

    （男：這班飛機延遲了三小時。我被告知我們將可在半小時後起飛。）

    W: That means the plane leaves at eleven twenty! I can't believe my ears.

    （女：意思是說這班飛機十一點二十分出發！我不能相信我的耳朵。）

    Q: What time is it now?（問題：現在的時間是？）

    (A)7:50.　　　　　(B)10:50.　　　　　(C)9:30.　　　　　(D)11:50.

    答案：(B)

9. W: What do you think of Beijing?（女：你認為北京如何？）

    M: I stayed in Beijing for a week. I really enjoyed the views there.

    （男：我在北京待了一星期。我真的很喜歡那邊的景色。）

    W: Then you came back home?（女：然後你就回家了？）

    M: A week is not enough! I spent another six days traveling around.

    （男：一星期不夠啦！我另外花了六天四處旅行。）

    Q: How long did the man spend traveling in Beijing?

    （問題：這位男士花了多少時間在北京旅行？）

    (A)For 13 days.（十三天。）　　　　　(B)For 2 weeks.（兩星期。）

    (C)For 6 days.（六天。）　　　　　(D)For 7 days.（七天。）

    答案：(A)

10. W: What is your lucky number, 8 or 6?（女：你的幸運數字是什麼，八或是六？）

    M: Neither. I like 7. It stands for eating food.

    （男：都不是。我喜歡七。它代表著吃東西。）

W: My lucky number is 3. It sounds like "rich".

（女：我的幸運數字是三。它聽起來像「有錢」。）

M: Why not choose 8? So many people regard it as their lucky number.

（男：為何不選八？那麼多人把它視為他們的幸運數字。）

W: I don't want to follow.（女：我不想跟潮流。）

Q: What number is the man's lucky number?（問題：這位男士的幸運數字是？）

(A)8.   (B)6.   (C)3.   (D)7.

答案：(D)

11. W: What a nice coat! How much is it?（女：多棒的一件外套啊！它多少錢？）

M: It costs at least 100 yuan.（男：它至少要一百元。）

W: Can I bargain?（女：我可以殺價嗎？）

M: Today is a special day and I can give you 10% discount.

（男：今天是個特別的日子我可以給妳九折優惠。）

Q: How much will the woman pay for the nice coat?

（問題：這位女士將付多少錢買這件好外套？）

(A)10 yuan.   (B)99 yuan.   (C)90 yuan.   (D)100 yuan.

答案：(C)

12. W: How long does it take you to go to school?（女：你上學要花多少時間？）

M: I walk for only five minutes from my home to the underground station. Then the underground takes me 20 minutes to reach Garden Station. I walk up to my school for another ten minutes.（男：從我家到地鐵站只要走五分鐘。然後地鐵花我二十分鐘到花園車站。我走到學校另外要十分鐘。）

W: It seems to be convenient, doesn't it?（女：似乎很便利，不是嗎？）

M: Yes, I am used to it.（男：是的，我習慣了。）

Q: How long does it take the boy from home to school?

（問題：這位男孩要花多少時間從家裡到學校？）

(A)25 min.（二十五分鐘）   (B)35 min.（三十五分鐘）

(C)15 min.（十五分鐘）   (D)20 min.（二十分鐘）

答案：(B)

13. W: Can you tell me your school telephone number as it has moved to a new place?（女：你可以告訴我你們學校的電話號碼嗎因為它搬到新地址了？）

M: Of course. It is 62131009.（男：當然。它是 62131009。）

W: It is the old number, isn't it?（女：這是老的號碼，不是嗎？）

M: I am so sorry. I am confused. The new number should be 61213008.

（男：我真抱歉。我搞混了。新的號碼應該是 61213008。）

Q: What is the new telephone number of the boy's school?

（問題：這位男孩的學校新的電話號碼是？）

(A)61213009.　　　　(B)62131009.　　　　(C)62131008.　　　　(D)61213008.

答案：(D)

14. W: I have put in 2 liters of milk. Then, I have to add 1 liter of water into the milk.（女：我放了兩公升牛奶進去。然後，我必須加一公升水到牛奶裡。）

　　M: I'm afraid that will be too much water. The instruction says that 4 liters of milk is mixed with 1 liter of water.

　　（男：我恐怕那樣會太多水。說明書說四公升牛奶混合一公升水。）

　　W: Let me have a check! Oh, you are right. Thank you!

　　（女：讓我撿查一下！。噢，你是對的。謝謝！）

　　Q: How much water should the girl add into the 2 liters of milk?

　　（問題：這位女孩應該加多少水到兩公升牛奶裡？）

　　(A)1 liter.（一公升）　　　　　　　　(B)2 liters.（兩公升）

　　(C)0.5 liter.（零點五公升）　　　　　(D)0.25 liter.（零點二五公升）

答案：(C)

15. W: Danny, the lottery number has come out. The numbers are 8, 17, 19, 22, 26, 29 and the lucky number is 32.

　　（女：丹尼，樂透號碼開出了。數字是 8, 17, 19, 22, 26, 29 而幸運號碼是 32。）

　　M: My lucky number is also 32. That's cool. And the others are 7, 18, 19, 23, 26 and the last is 29.（男：我的幸運號碼也是 32。真酷。其它的數字是 7, 18, 19, 23, 26 而最後一號是 29。）

　　W: You got a small prize. Congratulations.（女：你得到一個小獎。恭喜你。）

　　Q: How many numbers in the man's ticket are the same as the lottery numbers?（問題：這位男士的彩票中有多少個號碼是和樂透號碼相同的？）

　　(A)4.　　　　　(B)5.　　　　　(C)3.　　　　　(D)6.

答案：(A)

16. W: Today is already March 1st. Have you sent the letter to that company?

　　（女：今天已經是三月一日。你把那封信寄去那個公司了嗎？）

　　M: Of course. I sent it yesterday.（男：當然。我昨天就寄了。）

　　W: What was the letter about?（女：那封信是關於什麼的？）

　　M: In the letter, I told the company about the several parties during the next year of 2012.（男：在信中，我告訴該公司關於明年 2012 年的幾個派對。）

　　Q: What date was it the day before yesterday?（問題：前天的日期是？）

　　(A)March 1st.（三月一日）　　　　　　(B)Feb. 29rd.（二月二十九日）

　　(C)Feb. 28th.（二月二十八日）　　　　(D)Feb. 27th.（二月二十七日）

答案：(D)

Ⅲ、Listen to the passage and tell whether the following statements are true or false.

Why is one such a bad number? It is because when the date has this number in it, some bad things always happen. Let me give you some examples. In the midnight of September the twenty-first in Taiwan, the earthquake was very horrible. That night, there were about three thousand people who died in that accident. Many houses collapsed and the mountains moved.

為什麼一是那麼壞的一個數字？因為當日期有這個數字在裡面，總有些壞事發生。讓我給你一些例子。在九月二十一日台灣的午夜，那場地震很恐怖。那個夜晚，有大約三千人在那場意外中死去。很多房屋倒塌還發生走山。

America was attacked by terrorists on September 11 in 2001. The terrorists crashed into America's buildings with airplanes. The terrorists used airplanes to hit many tall buildings in America. There were bombs inside the buildings. When the airplanes hit the tall buildings, the tall buildings and the airplanes exploded. About six thousand people died. How terrible that was! I think the terrorists were crazy. People say that the American emergency number is 911, so the terrorists chose September 11 to attack America. There was a big typhoon on July 11 still in 2001 in Taiwan. Its name was Toraji. Many cities were flooded. Some people died because of landslides. These dates all contain the number "one". I really don't think "one" is a good or lucky number. So we have to be careful on the dates with this number.

美國在 2001 年九月十一日遭到恐怖份子攻擊。恐怖份子以飛機撞入美國的建築物。恐怖份子用飛機攻擊很多美國的高建築物。在建築物內有炸彈。當飛機撞到高建築物時，這高建築物和飛機就爆炸。大約六千人死亡。多麼恐怖啊！我認為恐怖份子們瘋了。人們說美國的緊急求救電話號碼是 911，所以恐怖份子選擇九月十一日攻擊美國。七月十一日同樣是 2001 年，在台灣有個大颱風。它的名字叫桃芝。很多都市都淹水。有些人因為土石流而死。這些日期都包含數字「一」。我真的不認為「一」是個好的或是幸運的數字。所以我們必須在有這個數字的日期小心點。

17. In the writer's opinion, one is an unlucky number.
（在筆者的看法中，一是個不幸運的數字。）
答案：(T 對)

18. The earthquake that happened in Taiwan in 2001 killed about 2,000 people.
（2001年發生在台灣的那場地震造成大約兩千人死亡。）
答案：(F 錯)

19. The terrorists attacked the U.S. on 9·11 because they thought one was really a bad number. （恐怖份子在九月十一日攻擊美國是因為他們認為一真的是個壞數字。）
答案：(F 錯)

20. The airplanes crashed into the tall buildings and luckily flew back to the air base. （飛機撞進了高建築物而後幸運地飛回了航空基地。）
答案：(F 錯)

21. On 7·11, a big typhoon attacked Taiwan in 2001.
（2001年，在七月十一日，一個大颱風襲及了台灣。）
答案：(T 對)

22. Some people died in the typhoon because the wind took them away.
（有些人在颱風中喪生，因為風把他們吹走了。）
答案：(F 錯)

23. According to the writer, January has the most days on which he will be quite careful.（根據筆者，一月有最多他會頗小心的日子。）
答案：(T 對)

IV、Listen to the passage and fill in the blanks with proper words.（聽短文,用最恰當的詞填空,每格限填一詞）（共 7 分）

A serious earthquake hit New Zealand, 30 km west of Christchurch early on Saturday morning. The quake, which had a depth of 20.5 miles, struck around 4:35 a.m. local time and was felt throughout much of the South Island and southern parts of the North Island.

星期六早上稍早，一場嚴重的地震襲及了紐西蘭基督城西方三十公里處。這場地震，深度二十點五英哩，發生於當地時間上午四點三十五分左右，在涵蓋南島大部分地區和北島的南部都可感受到。

Police in Christchurch, New Zealand's second-largest city with a population of about 350,000 people, closed the main business district of the city, with buildings falling into streets, damaging cars and blocking roads.

有大約三十五萬人口的紐西蘭第二大城基督城的警方關閉了市區主要的商業區,有建築物倒在路上，損壞了車輛且阻礙了道路。

The New Zealand government gave the degree as 7.4. The U.S. Geological Survey at first reported it at 7.4 but later changed its figure to 7.1.

紐西蘭政府判定其規模七點四級。美國地質評估機構起初公布它為七點四級，但之後更改它的數值為七點一。

The quake was felt as a long rolling motion lasting up to 40 seconds. The area was continuing to feel aftershocks as strong as degree 4.9.

這場地震感覺像是長的滾動持續長達四十秒。該地區持續感受到強達四點九級的餘震。

New Zealand scientists record around 14,000 earthquakes a year, of which around 20 top degree 5.0.

紐西蘭的科學家一年紀錄到大約一萬四千次地震，其中大約二十次超過五級。

The last serious earthquake was in 1968 when an earthquake measuring 7.1 killed three people on the South Island's West Coast.

上一次的嚴重地震是在 1968 年，一場規模七點一的地震在南島的西岸造成三人死

- A serious earthquake hit New Zealand at around __24__ a.m. local time.
（一場嚴重的地震當地時間上午 4:35 左右襲擊了紐西蘭。）
- Christchurch, New Zealand's second-largest city has a population of about __25__ people.
（基督城，紐西蘭第二大都市擁有約三十五萬人口。）
- The U.S. Geological Survey at first reported it at 7.4 but later changed its figure to __26__.
（美國地質評估機構起初公布它為七點四級，但之後更改它的數值為七點一。）
- The quake lasted up to __27__ seconds.（這場地震持續長達四十秒。）
- About __28__ earthquakes happen in New Zealand every year.
（在紐西蘭每年大約發生一萬四千次地震。）
- The last serious earthquake in New Zealand took place in __29__.
（上一次紐西蘭嚴重的地震發生於 1968 年。）
- __30__ people lost their lives in the last serious earthquake.
（三人在上一次的嚴重地震中喪生。）

24. 答案：4:35
25. 答案：350,000
26. 答案：7.1
27. 答案：40
28. 答案：14,000
29. 答案：1968
30. 答案：3

I、Listen and choose the right picture.（根據你所聽到的內容,選出相應的圖片。）（6分）

A   B   C

D   E   F   G

1. Keep quiet! You can't use mobile phones in the theatre.
   （保持安靜！你不可以在電影院裡使用行動電話。）
   答案：(A)

2. Can't you see the sign? It says no cycling.
   （你沒看見那個標示嗎？上面寫著不准騎腳踏車。）
   答案：(B)

3. Watch your steps! It's quite slippery here.（注意你的腳步！這裡相當的滑。）
   答案：(F)

4. Taking photos is not allowed in the museum.（在博物館裡拍照是不被允許的。）
   答案：(G)

5. Don't let your puppy enter the green grass.
   不要讓你的小狗進入草地。
   答案：(C)

6. You mustn't swim in the river. It's too dangerous.
   （你不可以在河裡游泳。太危險了。）

答案：(E)

II、Listen and choose the best response to the sentence you hear.（根據你所聽到的句子，選出最恰當的應答句。）（6分）

7. The sign tells us what we mustn't do. What sign is it?
    （這個標示告訴我們甚麼事不能做。那是甚麼標示？）
    (A)A direction sign.（方向標示。）
    (B)An information sign.（訊息標示。）
    (C)An instruction sign.（指示標示。）
    (D)A warning sign.（警告標示。）
    答案：(D)

8. Can I pick the flowers here?（我可以在這裡摘花嗎？）
    (A)Sorry, you mustn't.（抱歉，不行。）
    (B)Yes, you may.（是的，你也許可以。）
    (C)There are flowers in the park.（公園裡有花。）
    (D)Flowers are nice.（花很好看。）
    答案：(A)

9. Mum, I got an F for my English.（媽，我英文得了個F。）
    (A)I will take your advice.（我會採納你的建議。）
    (B)That's good.（那很好。）
    (C)You should study harder.（你該更努力一點。）
    (D)I think so.（應該吧。）
    答案：(C)

10. You have broken the school record for the 110-meter hurdle. Congratulations!
    （你已經打破110公尺跳欄的學校記錄。恭喜你！）
    (A)Thank you.（謝謝你。）   (B)Don't say so.（別這麼說。）
    (C)No, I don't.（不，我沒有。）   (D)That's all right.（沒關係。）
    答案：(A)

11. Let's plant more trees on Tree Planting Day!（我們在植樹節多種一些樹吧！）
    (A)Good idea.（好主意。）   (B)I think so, too.（我也這麼想。）
    (C)Yes, I will.（好的，我會。）   (D)I'm glad.（我很高興。）
    答案：(A)

12. How soon will you finish your work, Jim?（Jim，你多快可以完成你的工作？）
    (A)For at least one hour.（至少持續一小時。）
    (B)In one hour.（一小時以內。）

(C)At one o'clock.（一點。）

(D)By one hour.（差一小時。）

答案：(B)

Ⅲ、Listen to the dialogue and choose the best answer to the question you hear.（根據你所聽到的對話和問題,選出最恰當的答案。）（6分）

13. M: Can I smoke here?（M: 我可以在這裡抽菸嗎？）

　　W: Look at the sign on the wall. It says "No smoking".

　　　（W: 看看牆上的標示。上面寫著「禁止吸煙」）

　　Q: Can the man smoke here?（Q: 這個男人可以在這裡抽菸嗎?）

　　(A)Yes, he can.（是的，他可以。）　　(B)No, he can't.（不，他不可以。）

　　(C)Yes, he does.（是的，他抽菸。）　　(D)No, he doesn't.（不，他不抽菸。）

　　答案：(B)

14. M: Hi, this is John. How's everything going on with you?

　　　（M: 嗨，我是 John。妳好嗎?）

　　W: Shh... Don't talk loudly here. Haven't you seen the sign "Silence" over there? Everyone else is reading here.（W: 噓...別在這裡大聲說話。你沒看到那裡有個 "請安靜" 的標示嗎? 每個人都在這兒讀書。）

　　Q: Where does the dialogue probably take place?

　　　（Q: 這段對話大概發生在甚麼地方?）

　　(A)At home.（在家。）　　(B)In the hospital.（在醫院。）

　　(C)At the zoo.（在動物園。）　　(D)In the reading room.（在閱覽室。）

　　答案：(D)

15. M: Mrs Fraser, can we have an interview right now?

　　　（M: Fraser 女士，我們現在可以來進行面談嗎?）

　　W: Sure.（W: 當然可以。）

　　M: What job do you do?（M: 妳從事甚麼工作?）

　　W: I work for the SPCA. We protect the animals and help homeless animals find their new homes.

　　　（W: 我在 SPCA 工作。我們保護動物並幫助流浪動物找到牠們的新家。）

　　M: When did you start working as an SPCA officer?

　　　（M: 妳什麼時候開始擔任 SPCA 的工作人員?）

　　W: Three years ago.（W: 三年前。）

　　Q: What does the SPCA protect?（Q: SPCA 保護甚麼?）

　　(A)An SPCA officer.（SPCA 工作人員。）

　　(B)Homeless children.（無家可歸的兒童。）

(C)Homeless animals.（流浪動物。）

(D)Three years ago.（三年前。）

答案：(C)

16. M: How much are the apples?（M: 這些蘋果多少錢？）

W: 5 yuan a kilo.（W: 一公斤五元。）

M: What about the watermelon?（M: 西瓜呢？）

W: For the small ones, 10 yuan each and 15 yuan each for the big ones.

（W: 小的一個十元，大的一個十五元。）

M: Would you please give me two kilos of apples and one big watermelon?

（M: 請給我兩公斤蘋果和一個大西瓜。）

Q: How much will the man pay for the fruit?（Q: 這個男人花多少錢買水果？）

(A)10.   (B)15.   (C)20.   (D)25.

答案：(D)

17. W: What do you like to do in the future?（W: 你未來想做甚麼？）

M: I'd like to be a police officer. I want to catch thieves and help make the city safe. It's interesting. What about you?

（M: 我想當警察。我想逮捕小偷並協助維持城市的安全。這很有趣。妳呢？）

W: I want to be a doctor. I like to help others.

（W: 我想當醫生。我喜歡幫助他人。）

Q: What does the girl want to be in the future?

（Q: 女孩未來想當甚麼？）

(A)A police officer.（警察。）   (B)To catch thieves.（逮捕小偷。）

(C)To help others.（幫助其他人。）   (D)A doctor.（醫生。）

答案：(D)

18. W: Excuse me, what day is it today?（W: 抱歉，今天星期幾？）

M: It's Saturday.（M: 今天星期六。）

Q: What day was it the day before yesterday? （Q: 前天星期幾？）

(A)Wednesday.（星期三。）   (B)Thursday.（星期四。）

(C)Tuesday.（星期二。）   (D)Friday.（星期五。）

答案：(B)

IV、Listen to the dialogue and decide whether the following statements are True (T) or False (F). （判斷下列句子內容是否符合你所聽到的對話內容,符合的用"T"表示,不符合的用"F"表示。）（6 分）

Last Saturday Mr White and his wife went to the city centre. They spent a nice day in the downtown and got home very late. Mr White opened the front door and went into the house. It was very dark, so Mr White turned on the lights. On the way upstairs Mrs White said, "Listen, I can hear someone in the bedroom." So they went downstairs again and stood quietly outside the room, listening carefully. "Yes, you're right," said Mr White. "There are two boys. They are talking!" Then he called out, "Who is there?" But nobody answered. Mr White opened the door and quickly turned on the light. Then they burst out laughing. The radio was still on. "Oh, dear!" he said, "I forgot to turn off the radio this morning."

上星期六 White 先生和他的太太去市中心。他們一整天在鬧區玩得很開心，很晚才回家。White 先生打開前門進入屋內。屋裡非常暗，所以 White 先生把燈打開。White 太太要往樓梯走的時候，她說：「你聽，我聽見臥室裡有人。」於是他們又下樓，安靜的站在房間外面，仔細地聽。「是的，你是對的。」White 先生說。「裡面有兩個男孩，他們正在說話！」然後他大叫了出來：「是誰在那裡？」但是沒人回答。White 先生開了門，很快的把燈打開。結果他們都笑了出來。收音機還是開著的。「喔，親愛的！」他說，「今天早上我忘了關收音機了。」

19. Mr and Mrs White went to the city centre on Saturday.
（White 先生和太太星期六去市中心。）
答案：(T 對)

20. When Mr and Mrs White returned home late, it was very dark in the room.
（當 White 先生和太太很晚回家的時候，房間裡非常暗。）
答案：(T 對)

21. Mr and Mrs White's bedroom is on the ground floor.
（White 先生和太太的臥室在一樓。）
答案：(T 對)

22. On the way to the front door, they heard someone talking.
（在往前門的路上，他們聽見有人說話。）
答案：(F 錯)

23. Two boys broke into the house during the day time and stayed there.
（兩個男孩在白天的時候闖入他們家，並待在那兒。）
答案：(F 錯)

24. Mr White forgot to turn off the TV in the morning.
White 先生早上忘了關電視。
答案：(F 錯)

V、Listen and fill in the blanks. (根據你所聽到的內容,用適當的單詞完成下面的句子。每空格限填一詞。)(6分)

All students need to have good study habits. Good study habits are very important.

When you have them, you learn things quickly. You also remember them easily. For example, a living room is not a good place to study in, because it is too noisy. You need to study in a quiet place. A quiet place will help you concentrate (集中). When you study, don't think about other things at the same time. Only think about your homework. If you do this, you will make fewer mistakes. Every student should have good habits. If you do not have them, try to learn them. If yours are already good, try to make them better.

　　所有的學生都需要有好的讀書習慣。好的讀書習慣非常重要。只要你有了好的讀書習慣，你會學得很快。你也很容易記住這些習慣。舉例來說，客廳不是讀書的好地方，因為那兒太吵。你需要在安靜的地方讀書。安靜的地方可以幫助你集中精神。當你唸書的時候，不要同時想其它的事。只要想你的功課就好。這樣的話，你犯的錯就會比較少。每一個學生都應該有好的習慣。如果你沒有，試著學會。如果你的習慣已經很好了，試著讓它們更好。

25. Good study habits are very <u>important</u>.
    好的讀書習慣非常<u>重要</u>。

26. When you have good study habits, you learn things <u>quickly</u>.
    當你有了好的讀書習慣，你學東西會<u>很快</u>。

27. When you study, don't think about <u>other</u> things at the same time.
    當你讀書的時候，不要同時想<u>其它的</u>的事。

28. If you do this, you will make <u>fewer</u> mistakes.
    如果你這樣做的話，你犯的錯會<u>比較少</u>。

29. Every student should <u>have</u> good habits.
    每一個學生都應該<u>有</u>好的習慣。

30. If your study habits are already good, try to make them <u>better</u>.
    如果你的讀書習慣已經很好了，試著讓它們<u>更好</u>。

I、Listen and choose the right picture.

A.   B.   C.

D.   E.   F.   G.

1. Miss Green has a new car. So she drives to work every day and it saves her a lot of time.
   (格林小姐有一輛新車。所以她每天開車上班而省了很多時間。)
   答案：(F)

2. Mike, look at my new hat. It is a birthday present from my parents.
   (麥克，看看我的新帽子。它是我父母給我的生日禮物。)
   答案：(D)

3. When it snows here in winter, it is really happy to make a snowman.
   (當冬天這裡下雪時，堆雪人真的很快樂。)
   答案：(G)

4. Mary always helps her mother do the housework and now she is doing some washing.
   (瑪莉總是幫助她母親做家事而現在她正在洗東西。)
   答案：(E)

5. Tom and Tim are twins. They are always together after school.
   (湯姆和提姆是雙胞胎。他們放學後總是在一起。)
   答案：(B)

6. I like working with children so I'd like to work as a nurse in a children's hospital.
   (我喜歡和小孩子們一起工作所以我想在兒童醫院當一名護士。)
   答案：(A)

II、Listen to the dialogue and choose the best answer to the question you hear.

---

7. M: Will you leave at 6.00 or a quarter past six in the morning, Miss Green?
   （男：妳將會在早上六點或六點十五分離開，格林小姐？）
   W: Neither. I'll leave at five to seven. (女：都不是。我將在六點五十五分離開。)
   Q: What time will Miss Green leave? (問題：格林小姐幾點將離開？)
   (A)At 5.45a.m. (上午五點四十五分。)　　　　(B)At 6.15a.m. (上午六點十五分。)
   (C)At 6.45a.m. (上午六點四十五分。)　　　　(D)At 6.55a.m. (上午六點五十五分。)
   答案：(D)

8. W: Look, Jim. We can park our car here. (女：你看，吉姆。我們可以把我們的車停在這裡。)
   M: Great. Then we don't need to worry about the time to go around.
   　（男：太好了。那麼我們就不必擔心四處逛逛的時間。
   Q: Which sign are they talking about? (問題：他們正在談論的是什麼標誌？)

   (A)　　　　　　　　(B)　　　　　　　　(C)　　　　　　　　(D)

   答案：(B)

9. M: Alice, why are you at home? Didn't you go for a picnic?
   　（男：艾莉絲，妳為什麼在家裡？妳沒有去野餐嗎？）
   W: No, it was raining hard and I have to go back home, watching TV.
   　（女：沒，雨下得很大而我必須回家，看電視。）
   Q: Why does Alice have to stay home? (問題：為什麼艾莉絲必須待在家裡？)
   (A)Because she was late for the bus. (因為她沒趕上巴士。)
   (B)Because the picnic is terrible. (因為野餐很可怕。)
   (C)Because the TV play is interesting. (因為電視節目很有趣。)
   (D)Because it was raining hard. (因為雨下得很大。)
   答案：(D)

10. W: How did your parents like their holiday in Hainan?
    　（女：你的父母喜歡他們在海南的假期嗎？）
    M: My father thought there were too many people there, but my mother liked it.
    　（男：我父親認為那邊人太多，但我母親滿喜歡那邊。）
    Q: Did the boy's parents like the holiday? (問題：這位男孩的父母喜歡這個假期嗎？)
    (A)Yes, both of them liked it. (是的，他們都喜歡。)
    (B)No, neither of them liked it. (不，他們都不喜歡。)

(C)His father didn't like it, but his mother did. (他父親不喜歡，但他母親喜歡。)

(D)His mother didn't like it, but his father did. (他母親不喜歡，但他父親喜歡。)

答案：(C)

11. M: What are you going to have for dinner today? (男：妳今天晚餐將要吃什麼？)

W: I have no idea. (女：我毫無頭緒。)

M: Shall we have some fish? (男：那我們要不要吃一些魚？)

W: No. Let's have some meat. (女：不。讓我們吃一些肉吧。)

M: OK. That's a good idea. (男：好。那是個好主意。)

Q: What are they going to have for dinner today? (問題：他們今天晚餐將要吃什麼？)

(A)To have some fish. (吃一些魚)　　　　(B)To have some meat. (吃一些肉)

(C)To have some vegetables. (吃一些蔬菜)　　(D)To have some chicken. (吃一些雞肉)

答案：(B)

12. W: How about going to the city center? (女：去市政中心怎麼樣？)

M: I'd love to, but I have a lot of things to do. I am too busy these days.
　　(男：我很想去，但我有一堆事情要做。我這幾天太忙了。)

Q: What does the boy mean? (問題：這位男孩的意思是？)

(A)He has been to the city center before. (他以前去過市政中心。)

(B)He is too busy. (他太忙。)

(C)He doesn't like the city center. (他不喜歡市政中心。)

(D)He will not go to the city center. (他不去市政中心。)

答案：(D)

13. M: Did you watch the football match last night, Ann? (男：妳有看昨晚的足球賽嗎，安？)

W: No, I looked after my brother in the hospital. (女：沒有，我在醫院照顧我兄弟。)

Q: Where was Ann last night? (問題：安昨晚在哪裡？)

(A)At home. (在家)　　　　　　　　　　(B)In the hospital. (在醫院)

(C)In the library. (在圖書館)　　　　　　(D)On the playground. (在遊戲場)

答案：(B)

14. M: What can I do for you? (男：有我可以為您效勞的嗎？)

W: I have a fever and feel terrible. (女：我發燒了覺得很不舒服。)

M: Let me see. Oh, you just have a cold. Take some medicine, and you will be OK soon.
　　(男：讓我看看。噢，妳只是感冒了。服一些藥，妳很快就會好了。)

W: Thank you. (女：謝謝。)

Q: What's the matter with the girl? (問題：這位女孩怎麼了？)

(A)She has a cold. (她感冒了。)　　　　　(B)She has toothache. (她牙痛。)

(C)She has a cough. (她咳嗽。)　　　　　(D)She has a stomachache. (她胃痛。)

答案：(A)

15. M: We'll have summer holidays next month. Where are you going?
　　(男：我們下個月要放暑假。妳要去哪裡呢？)

W: I'm going to Chongqing. (女：我要去重慶。)

M: How are you going there? (男：妳要怎麼去那裡？)

W: By plane. (女：搭飛機。)

M: I think it's cheaper to go there by train. (男：我想，搭火車去會比較便宜。)

W: Maybe next time. I've booked the air ticket. (女：或許下次吧。我已經訂了機票。)

Q: How is the girl going to Chongqing? (問題：這位女孩要怎麼去重慶？)

(A)By bus. (搭巴士)　(B)By train. (搭火車)　(C)By plane. (搭飛機)　(D)By ship. (搭船)

答案：(C)

16. W: Dad, I'll be late for school. Could you drive me to school today?

　　(女：爸，我上學要遲到了。你今天可否載我去學校？)

M: Sure. But you should get up earlier next time. (男：當然。但是妳下次應該早點起床。)

W: Thank you. I will. (女：謝謝。我會的。)

Q: What's the relationship between the two speakers? (問題：這兩位對話者的關係是？)

(A)Teacher and student. (老師與學生)　　　(B)Husband and wife. (丈夫與太太)

(C)Father and daughter. (父女)　　　　　(D)Mother and son. (母子)

答案：(C)

Ⅲ、Listen to the passage and tell whether the following statements are true or false.

Stephen Hawking was born in Oxford, England on January 8, 1942. He went to school in St Albans. After leaving school, Hawking went first to Oxford University where he studied physics, and then he went on studying in Cambridge University. As he himself says, he didn't work hard. He was a lazy student and did very little work. However, he still got good marks.

史蒂芬霍金 1942 年 1 月 8 日出生於英國牛津。他在聖奧本斯上學。離開學校後，霍金首先去了牛津大學，在那裡學習物理，然後他去劍橋大學繼續就讀，據他自己所說，他沒有用功。他是個懶學生且做很少功課。然而，他仍然拿到好成績。

At the age of 20, he first noticed something was wrong with him. His mother was very worried and took him to see the doctor. He was sent to the hospital for tests. He was ill. The doctor said he would die before he was 23.

在二十歲時，他初次注意到他有什麼不對勁。他的母親很擔憂而帶他去看醫師。他被送去醫院做檢查。他生病了。醫師說他將會在二十三歲前死去。

At first, he became very sad and disappointed. After coming out of the hospital, he suddenly realized that life was beautiful. Later he married, found a job and had three children. He also went on with some of the most important scientific researches.

起初，他變得很悲傷且失望。從醫院出來之後，他忽然領悟到人生是美好的。之後他結婚了，找到工作且生了三個小孩。他也繼續了某些最重要的科學研究。

Today, Hawking still works at Cambridge University as a professor. He strongly believes that his story shows that nobody, however bad his situation is, should lose hope. "Life is not fair," he once said. "You just have to do the best you can in your own situation."

今天，霍金仍然在劍橋大學當教授。他強烈地相信他的故事顯示出無論一個人的境況有多糟，沒有人應該失去希望。「人生不是公平的」他曾說。「你只要在你的狀況下盡力而為。」

17. Stephen Hawking was born in Oxford and once studied in Cambridge University.
   (史蒂芬霍金出生於牛津而且曾在劍橋大學就讀。)
   答案：(T 對)

18. As a university student, Stephen Hawking worked hard and got good marks.
   (身為大學生，史蒂芬霍金很用功且得到好成績。)
   答案：(F 錯)

19. Stephen Hawking first noticed something was wrong with him when he was 23.
   (史蒂芬霍金初次注意到他有什麼不對勁是在他二十三歲時。)
   答案：(F 錯)

20. Stephen Hawking changed his life attitude after he came out of the hospital.
   (史蒂芬霍金在從醫院出來之後改變了他的人生態度。)
   答案：(T 對)

21. Later Stephen Hawking married and there were three people in his family.
   (之後史蒂芬霍金結婚了而他的家裡有三個人。)
   答案：(F 錯)

22. Stephen Hawking did some scientific researches and now works as a professor at Oxford University. (史蒂芬霍金做了某些科學研究而現在在牛津大學當教授。)
   答案：(F 錯)

23. From the passage, we know that we shouldn't lose hope even in a bad situation.
   (透過此短文，我們知道即使在很糟的狀況下，我們也不應該失去希望。)
   答案：(T 對)

IV、Listen to the passage and fill in the blanks.

This message is for Marco Daniel.
這篇留言是給馬可丹尼爾。

My name's David Dolby. I'm sorry I missed your call. I understand that you want some information about the volleyball club. The club meets once a week, on Wednesday evening. Sometimes there are matches on Sunday morning, but those are just for our team players. Our meetings begin at eight, and are about two hours long, so we finish at ten. People like to get home in time for the 10:15 sports program on television. We meet in the Jubilee Hall in Park Lane, behind High Street. The hall doesn't have very good heating, so you'll need to bring a coat to put on afterwards. It's also quite expensive to rent, so our players pay ￡2.75 each week. I hope this answers all your questions and we'll be very pleased to see you at our next meeting!

我的名字是大衛杜比。很抱歉漏接了您的電話。我明白你想要一些關於排球社的資訊。該社團一星期聚會一次，在星期三晚上。有時候星期天早上會有球賽，但是那只是針對我們的球隊選手。我們的聚會八點開始，大約兩小時長，所以我們在十點結束。人們喜歡及時回家收看電視上十點十五分的體育節目。我們在公園路的朱比利堂聚會，在主要大街後面。該堂沒有很好的暖氣，所以您需要帶外套來以便事後穿上。它的租金也頗貴的，所以我們的選手每星期付二點七五英鎊。我希望這回答了您所有的問題，且我們會很高興在我們下一次的聚會見到您！

- Marco Daniel wants some information about the __24__ club.
  馬可丹尼爾想要一些關於排球社的資訊。

- The members in the club meet every __25__ evening.
  該社團的社員每星期三晚上聚會。

- Matches on Sunday morning are just for their __26__ players.
  星期天早上的球賽只是針對他們的球隊選手。

- The meetings begin at __27__, and are about two hours long.
  聚會八點開始，大約兩小時長。

- People like to get home before 10:15 to watch the __28__ program on TV.
  人們喜歡在十點十五分之前回家收看電視上的體育節目。

- They meet in the Jubilee Hall in Park Lane, behind __29__ Street.
  他們在公園路的朱比利堂聚會，在主要大街後面。

- The hall doesn't have very good heating, so Marco Daniel should take a __30__ to put on afterwards.
  該堂沒有很好的暖氣，所以馬可丹尼爾應該帶一件外套來之後穿上。

24. 答案：volleyball (排球)
25. 答案：Wednesday (星期三)
26. 答案：team (球隊)
27. 答案：eight/8 (八)
28. 答案：sports (體育)
29. 答案：High（英國各城市主要大街的普遍名稱）
30. 答案：coat (外套)

Unit 7

I、Listen and choose the right picture.（根據你所聽到的內容，選出相應的圖片。）（6分）

A.　　　　　　　　B.　　　　　　　　C.

D.　　　　　E.　　　　　F.　　　　　G.

1. We are taking a lot of presents with us today because I am hurrying to my grandparents' with my parents. (我們今天帶了好多禮物，因為我趕著跟我爸媽去祖父母家。)
   答案：(C)

2. The Lis are having a big dinner together happily.
   (Lis 全家很開心的在一起吃一頓盛大的晚餐。)
   答案：(B)

3. Pigeons on the People's Square are not afraid of people because Shanghainese are always very friendly to them.
   (人民廣場上的鴿子不怕人，因為上海人對牠們總是很和善。)
   答案：(G)

4. Do people still enjoy the beautiful moon on the night of the Mid-autumn Festival nowadays?
   (現在的人們仍然會在中秋節晚上欣賞漂亮的月亮嗎？)
   答案：(A)

5. The students are chatting around the camp-fire at the campsite.
   (學生們在營地圍著營火聊天。)
   答案：(E)

6. Would you like to go to the beach with me tomorrow?
   (你明天想跟我去海邊嗎？)

答案：(F)

II、Listen to the dialogue and choose the best answer to the question you hear.（根據你所聽到的對話和問題，選出最恰當的答案。）（10 分）

7. W: Which subject do you prefer, music or sports, Sidney?

   (W: Sidney，你比較喜歡哪一科，音樂還是運動？)

   M: I prefer music to sports. (M:我喜歡音樂多過於運動。)

   Question: Which subject does Sidney like better? (問題：Sidney 比較喜歡哪一科？)

   (A)Maths. (數學。)　　　　　　　　　　(B)Sports. (運動。)

   (C)Music. (音樂。)　　　　　　　　　　(D)Science. (科學。)

   答案：(C)

8. M: The physics problem is very difficult, Mum? (M: 媽，物理問題非常難呢。)

   W: Yes, it may be. Would you like me to help you, David?

   (W: 可能吧。David，你希望我幫你嗎？)

   M: No, thanks, Mum. I'll try to do it myself. (M: 媽，不用了，謝謝。我自己試試看。)

   Question: Why doesn't Tom want his mother to help him?

   (問題：為什麼 Tom 不讓她母親幫他？)

   (A)Tom wants to do it by himself. (Tom 想自己做。)

   (B)Tom doesn't think it's so hard. (Tom 不認為那很困難。)

   (C)Tom is very clever. (Tom 非常聰明。)

   (D)His mother can't work it out. (他母親沒辦法解出來。)

   答案：(A)

9. W: Where have you been? I've looked for you everywhere! (W: 你去哪兒了？我到處找你！)

   M: I was at the school library. I borrowed some books there.

   (M: 我在學校圖書館。我在那兒借了幾本書。)

   W: Are you going to read these books now? (W: 你現在要讀那些書嗎？)

   M: No. I'm going to play basketball with my classmates. (M: 不。我要跟我同學去打籃球。)

   Question: Where was the boy? (問題：那男孩之前在哪裡？)

   (A)At the school. (在學校。)　　　　　　(B)At the school library. (在學校圖書館。)

   (C)On the playground. (在遊戲場。)　　　(D)At home. (在家。)

   答案：(B)

10. W: Can I help you? (W: 我能為你服務嗎？)

    M: Yes. I bought this radio two days ago, but it doesn't work. I'd like to change it for another

    one. (M: 好。我兩天前買了這台收音機，但是它壞了。我想要換另一台。)

    W: Yes. Of course. Have you got your receipt? (W: 當然。你帶了收據嗎？)

    M: Yes. Here you are. (M: 帶了。在這兒。)

    W: Thank you. Just a moment, please. (W: 謝謝。請稍候。)

Question: What will probably happen finally? (問題：最後可能會發生甚麼事？)

(A)The man got a new receipt. (那男人拿到一張新的收據。)

(B)The man got his radio repaired. (那男人把收音機送修了。)

(C)The man got a new radio. (那男人拿到一台新的收音機。)

(D)The man left there without a radio. (那男人沒帶收音機就離開那兒了。)

答案：(C)

11. W: Is this bike yours, Mike? (W: Mike，這是你的腳踏車嗎？)

    M: No, it isn't. (M: 不，它不是。)

    W: Whose bike is it, do you know? (W: 你知道這是誰的腳踏車嗎？)

    M: Perhaps, it's my sister's. (M: 可能是我姊姊的。)

    Question: Who is the owner of the bike? (問題：誰這這輛腳踏車的主人？)

    (A)Mike.   (B)Mike's mother. (Mike 的母親。)

    (C)Mike's sister. (Mike 的姊姊。)   (D)Mike's father. (Mike 的父親。)

答案：(C)

12. W: What are you doing, George? (W: George 你在做甚麼？)

    M: I ... I'm drawing, Miss Li. (M: 李老師，我...我在畫圖。)

    W: Oh, yes. What a nice car! But you'd better do it after class.

       (W: 喔，對。多棒的一輛車。但是你最好下課後再畫。)

    M: I'm sorry, Miss Li. (M: Li 老師，對不起。)

    Question: When does the dialogue happen? (問題：這段對話甚麼時候發生？)

    (A)Before class. (上課前。)   (B)During the class. (課堂上。)

    (C)After class. (下課後。)   (D)In the classroom. (在教室裡。)

答案：(B)

13. W: Do you often go to school by bus, Peter? (W: Peter，你常搭公車上學嗎？)

    M: No, never. I usually go on my bike. But if it rains, my father drives me there.

       (M: 從來沒有。我通常騎腳踏車。如果下雨的話，我爸爸開車載我去。)

    Question: How does Peter go to school on a rainy day? (問題：下雨天 Peter 怎麼去上學？)

    (A)By bus. (搭公車。)   (B)By bike. (騎腳踏車。)

    (C)By car. (搭車。)   (D)On foot. (走路。)

答案：(C)

14. M: Excuse me, how can I get to the museum? (M: 不好意思，我該怎麼去博物館？)

    W: Take a No.71 Bus. It will take you twenty minutes to get there. And the bus stop is five minutes' walk from here. (W: 搭七十一號公車。到那裡要花二十分鐘。這裡到公車站要走五分鐘。)

    Question: How long will it take the man to get to the museum?

       (問題：那男人去博物館要花多久時間？)

    (A)Five minutes. (五分鐘。)   (B)Fifteen minutes. (十五分鐘。)

    (C)Twenty minutes. (二十分鐘。)   (D)Twenty-five minutes. (二十五分鐘。)

答案：(D)

15. W: Hi, Li Ming, did you take part in the school sports meeting yesterday?

   (W: 嗨，Li Ming，你昨天參加學校運動會了嗎？)

   M: Yes, I took part in the 400-metre race. I was third and Wang Pen was second.

   (M: 是的。我參加四百公尺賽跑。我第三名，Wang Pen 第二名。)

   Question: Who runs fastest in the race? (問題：誰在比賽中跑得最快？)

   (A)We don't know from this passage. (我們無法從這段對話中知道。)

   (B)The girl. (那女孩。)

   (C)Wang Pen.

   (D)Li Ming.

   答案：(A)

16. W: Does either of you want a ticket for the science report?

   (W: 你們任何一個想要科學報告的門票嗎？)

   M: Why not? Would you like to go? (M: 為什麼不？你想去嗎？)

   W: I'd like to, but I've got a lot of things to do for the coming exams.

   (W: 我想，但是我為了下一場考試還有好多事要做。)

   Question: Why isn't the woman going to the science report?

   (問題：那女人為什麼不去科學報告？)

   (A)She's too busy to go.(她太忙以至於不能去)

   (B)She's not interested in it. (她沒興趣。)

   (C)She hasn't got any tickets. (她沒有票。)

   (D)She's ill. (她生病了。)

   答案：(A)

Ⅲ、Listen to the passage and decide whether the following statements are True (T) or False (F). (判斷下列句子內容是否符合你所聽到的短文內容，符合的用 T 表示，不符合的用 F 表示。) (7 分）

Kelly always wanted to be a scientist. She was interested in maths and physics. She hoped to work in space one day. "I will discover something important in the future," she often told herself.

Kelly 一直想當科學家。她對數學、物理很感興趣。她希望有一天能在太空工作。「未來我將發現重要的事。」她常常告訴自己。

Every evening, Kelly went out with her dog to look at the stars. One night, she saw a strange, coloured light moving across the sky.

Kelly 每天晚上帶她的狗去外面看星星。一天晚上，她看見一道奇特的彩色光芒橫越天空。

"It can't be a star," she thought. "It's too bright. It must be a spaceship! I'm going to see it!"

She walked quickly towards the light.

「那不可能是星星。」她想，「那太亮了。那一定是太空船！我要去看它。」
她很快地走向那道光。

"The people in the spaceship will want to talk to me. Can they speak our language? Will I be able to understand them? Are they lost?"

「太空船裡的人會想跟我說話。他們會說我們的語言嗎？我會了解他們嗎？他們迷路了嗎？」

The spaceship landed a few metres in front of Kelly and the door slowly opened. Suddenly, Kelly's dog ran towards the spaceship. Kelly cried, "This can't be true!" Two huge dogs stood at the door of the spaceship. The visitors from space were dogs! They said a few words to Kelly's dog. Kelly's dog looked at Kelly and then turned and ran into the spaceship. Then the spaceship was gone.

那艘太空船在 Kelly 前方數公尺降落，門緩慢地打開了。忽然間，Kelly 的狗跑向太空船。Kelly 大叫：「這不可能是真的。」兩隻大狗站在太空船的門口。從太空來的訪客是狗！他們對 Kelly 的狗說了幾句話。Kelly 的狗看看 Kelly，然後轉頭跑進太空船。然後太空船就消失了。

17. Kelly always wanted to be an astronaut to work in space one day.
    (Kelly 希望有一天當一名在太空工作的太空人。)
    答案：(F 錯)

18. Kelly always thought that she would discover some important things in the future.
    (Kelly 總是想著她未來將發現重要的事物。)
    答案：(T 對)

19. One night, Kelly saw a strange, coloured light moving across the sky in the park with her dog.
    (一天晚上，Kelly 跟她的狗在公園看見一道奇特的彩色光芒橫越天空。)
    答案：(T 對)

20. Kelly thought the light was from a spaceship. (Kelly 認為那道光是來自太空船。)
    答案：(T 對)

21. The spaceship landed a few metres in front of Kelly. (太空船在 Kelly 前方數公尺處降落。)
    答案：(T 對)

22. Kelly was able to understand what the aliens in the spaceship said.
    (Kelly 能夠了解太空船上的外星人說什麼。)
    答案：(F 錯)

23. Kelly's dog went up to the spaceship and never came back again.
    (Kelly 的狗跑上太空船，再也沒回來了。)
    答案：(T 對)

Jack: Hello, Mrs. Hu. What's in your hand?

(Jack: 哈囉，Hu 太太。你手裡的是甚麼？)

Mrs. Hu: Oh! Hello, Jack. It's an interesting magazine. It has a report about the future.

(Hu 太太: 喔！哈囉，Jack。這是一本很有趣的雜誌。它有一篇關於未來的報導。)

Jack: Does it say we will live on the moon or things like that?

(Jack: 它是不是說我們將來會住在月球上之類的事情？)

Mrs. Hu: Well, yes. And it also says here people will live in glass houses by the year 2100.

(Hu 太太: 嗯，對。它也說 2100 年我們這裡的人將住在玻璃屋裡。)

Jack: Glass houses? That sounds interesting!

(Jack: 玻璃屋？聽起來好有趣！)

Mrs. Hu: And medicine will cure every illness in the future. People will never get sick.

(Hu 太太: 而且未來的藥物將治癒每一種疾病。人們將不再生病。)

Jack: Then, we'll live longer. What about spaceships? Does it say anything about space?

(Jack: 那麼我們就活得更長了。那麼太空船呢？它提到太空船了嗎？)

Mrs. Hu: Yes, of course! In the future, we'll have holidays in space and live on other planets.

(Hu 太太:當然有！未來，我們將在太空渡假，並且住在其他星球上。)

Jack: It sounds crazy, but fun! I hope it will come true.

(Jack: 這聽起來有點瘋狂，但是太好玩了！我希望那會成真。)

Mrs. Hu: It also says trains are going to be faster. People will travel by train rather than by plane.

(Hu 太太: 他也說火車將會更快。人們將會搭火車而不搭飛機旅行。)

Jack: That's quite strange. We have to travel by plane if we want to go to another country. And planes go much faster than trains!

(Jack: 那太奇怪了。如果我們想去其他國家，我們必須搭飛機旅行。而且飛機比火車快多了！)

Mrs. Hu: Yes, you are right. But planes use too much petrol and the report says we'll run out of it in the future.

(Hu 太太: 對。但是飛機用太多石油，報導說未來我們將用光石油。)

Jack: I see. It's important to protect our environment from now on. Then we'll have a bright future.

(Jack: 我知道了。從現在起保護我們的環境很重要。這樣我們就會有個光明的未來。)

Mrs. Hu: I agree with you.

(Hu 太太: 我同意。)

- People will live on the __24__. They will also live in __25__ houses by the year 2100. (人們將住在___上。他們也將在 2100 年住在____屋裡。)
- __26__ will cure every illness in the future and people will live __27__ than ever. (____將

治癒每一種疾病，人們將活得比以前＿＿。)

- People will have __28__ in space and live on other __29__. (人們將在太空＿＿＿，並住在其他的＿＿＿。)
- People will run out of energy sources in the future so people must try to protect the __30__. (未來人們將耗盡能源，所以人們必須試著保護＿＿＿。)

24. 答案：moon (月球)
25. 答案：glass (玻璃)
26. 答案：Medicine (藥物)
27. 答案：longer (更長/較長的)
28. 答案：holidays (假日)
29. 答案：planets (星球)
30. 答案：environment (環境)

Unit 8

I 、Listen and choose the right picture. (根據你所聽到的內容，選出相應的圖片)（5分）

A.　　　　　　　　B.　　　　　　　　C.

D.　　　　　　　　E.　　　　　　　　F.

1. I went to the zoo this morning. The elephants there were really lovely.
（我今天早上去動物園。那裡的大象真的好可愛。）
答案：(B)

2. Don't cry, Judy! I can help you.
（Judy，不要哭。我可以幫你。）
答案：(C)

3. Nice to meet you, Andy!
（Andy，很高興認識你。）
答案：(D)

4. Excuse me, may I have a ticket, please?
（不好意思，請給我一張票好嗎？）
答案：(E)

5. We can ask policemen for help when we have any trouble.
   （當我們有任何麻煩的時候，我們可以向警察求救。）
   答案：(F)

II、Listen and choose the right word you hear in each sentence.（根據你所聽到的句子，選出正確的單字。）(5分)

---

6. Long ago, Stone Age people ate raw meat.
   （很久以前，石器時代的人吃生肉。）
   (A)meet（遇見）   (B)meat（肉類）
   (C)met（遇見）（過去式）   (D)meeting（會議）
   答案：(B)

7. Break an egg and fry the two sides please.
   （打一顆蛋，並且請把兩面煎熟。）
   (A)friend（朋友）   (B)fry（炒、炸）
   (C)fried（炒、炸）（過去式）   (D)frog（青蛙）
   答案：(B)

8. There are seventeen girls and twenty boys in our class.
   （我們班上有十七個女生、二十個男生。）
   (A)seventy（七十）   (B)seven（七）
   (C)seventeen（十七）   (D)seventh（第七）
   答案：(C)

9. What's the price for these apples?
   這些蘋果要多少錢？
   (A)prize（獎）   (B)praise（讚美）
   (C)please（請）   (D)price（價錢）
   答案：(D)

10. Taste this soup. It's delicious.（嚐嚐這碗湯。它非常美味。）
    (A)soup（湯）   (B)soap（肥皂）
    (C)supper（晚餐）   (D)super（超級）
    答案：(A)

11. What would you like for dinner tonight? Rice or noodles?
（今晚的晚餐你想吃甚麼？飯還是麵？）
(A)Yes, I would like some rice.（是的，我想要一些米飯。）
(B)Yes, I would like some noodles.（是的，我想要一些麵。）
(C)I don't want any dumplings.（我不要餃子。）
(D)Rice, please.（請給我米飯。）
答案：(D)

12. Where did you buy the fish, Mum?（媽，你在哪裡買這條魚？）
(A)In the supermarket, at the meat section.（在超級市場的肉品區。）
(B)In the supermarket, at the frozen food section.（在超級市場的冷凍食物區。）
(C)In the market, in the seafood stall.（在市場的海鮮攤位。）
(D)In the market, in the fruit stall.（在市場的水果攤位。）
答案：(C)

13. How much do these apples cost?（這些蘋果要價多少？）
(A)24 yuan altogether.（一共二十四元。）
(B)I bought a box of apples.（我買了一盒蘋果。）
(C)I don't like apples at all.（我一點也不喜歡吃蘋果。）
(D)Let's have some apples.（我們來吃點蘋果吧。）
答案：(A)

14. Let's hold a birthday party for your grandmother! It'll be her seventieth birthday next Thursday.
（讓我們來為你的祖母舉辦生日派對吧！下星期四就是她七十歲生日。）
(A)That's a good idea.（那是個好主意。）
(B)Thank you very much.（非常感謝你。）
(C)Nice to meet you.（很高興認識你。）
(D)Let's go to the supermarket.（我們去超級市場吧。）
答案：(A)

15. How much ice cream have you bought, Dad?（老爸，你買了多少冰淇淋？）

    (A)I have bought some ice cream in the supermarket.
    （我已經在超級市場買了一些冰淇淋。）

    (B)I have bought two boxes of ice cream.（我已經買了兩盒冰淇淋。）

    (C)I have bought my daughter some ice cream.（我已經幫我女兒買了一些冰淇淋。）

    (D)I bought the ice cream yesterday.（我昨天買了冰淇淋。）

    答案：(B)

IV、Listen to the dialogue and choose the best answer to the question you hear.
（根據你所聽到的對話和問題，選出最恰當的答案。）（5 分）

---

16. W: Would you like some coffee or tea?（W: 你想要咖啡還是茶？）

    M: I love both. But it's too hot today. I'd like some cold water.
    （M: 我兩個都喜歡。但是今天太熱了。我想要冰水。）

    Question: What does the man want to drink?
    （問題：男人想喝甚麼？）

    (A)Water.（水。）

    (B)Cola.（可樂。）

    (C)Coffee.（咖啡。）

    (D)Tea.（茶。）

    答案：(A)

17. M: How much money have you got?（M: 你有多少錢？）

    W: I've got twenty-five yuan. And you?（W: 我有二十五元。你呢？）

    M: I've got twelve yuan. I know Ben has got twenty yuan.
    （M: 我有十二元。我知道 Ben 有二十元。）

    Question: How much money have the children got altogether?
    （問題：這些孩子們一共有多少錢？）

    (A)￥45.（四十五元。）

    (B)￥57.（五十七元。）

    (C)￥37.（三十七元。）

    (D)￥75.（七十五元。）

    答案：(B)

18. M: What do you need to buy from the supermarket, Mum?
      （M: 媽，你需要在超級市場買甚麼？）

   W: I need some ice cream, some fish and some soft drinks from the supermarket.
      （W: 我需要在超級市場買一些冰淇淋、一些魚和一些碳酸飲料。）

   Question: Which section won't Mum go to in the supermarket?
      （問題：媽媽不會去超級市場裡的哪個區？）

   (A)Meat section.（肉品區。）

   (B)Seafood section.（海鮮區。）

   (C)Drink section.（飲料區。）

   (D)Frozen food section.（冷凍食物區。）

   答案：(A)

19. M: Do you want some dessert after dinner?（M: 晚餐後你想要來些甜點嗎？）

   W: Yes, I'd love to.（W: 好，我要。）

   M: Would you like ice cream or pudding?（M: 你喜歡冰淇淋還是布丁？）

   W: I'd love pudding.（W: 我想要布丁。）

   M: What would you like on your pudding? Mango or strawberry?
      （M: 你想要怎樣的布丁？芒果還是草莓。）

   W: Strawberry, please.（W: 請給我草莓。）

   Question: What kind of dessert will the girl have?
      （問題：女孩想要怎樣的甜點？）

   (A)Mango ice cream.（芒果冰淇淋。）

   (B)Mango pudding.（芒果布丁。）

   (C)Strawberry ice cream. 草莓冰淇淋。）

   (D)Strawberry pudding.（草莓布丁。）

   答案：(D)

20. M: What would you like to have for dinner tonight?
      （M:今天晚上的晚餐你想吃甚麼？）

   W: I want to have some dumplings and Beijing Duck.
      （W: 我想吃餃子和北京烤鴨。）

   M: OK. We can go to ...（M: 好。我們可以去...）

   Question: What kind of restaurant will they probably go to?
      （問題：他們可能會去怎樣的餐廳？）

   (A)A pizza café.（披薩餐廳。）

   (B)A fast food restaurant.（速食餐廳。）

(C)The KFC.（肯德基。）

(D)A Chinese restaurant.（中國餐廳。）

答案：(D)

V、Listen to the passage and decide whether the following statements are True (T) or False (F).（判斷下列句子內容是否符合你所聽到的短文內容，符合的用 T 表示，不符合的用 F 表示。）(5分)

Pizza is a kind of popular food.（披薩是一種很受歡迎的食物。）

It has a long history.（它有悠久的歷史。）

Most people think it comes from Italy.（大部分的人們認為它來自義大利。）

The world's first pizza restaurant is in Naples, a famous city in Italy.

（世界上第一家披薩餐廳是在那不勒斯，一個著名的義大利城市。）

It opened more than 100 years ago.（餐廳在一百多年前開幕。）

Modern pizza was first made by a person named Refael Esposito in the 1880s.

（現代披薩是在 1880 年代由一位叫做 Rafael Esposito 的人首先製作的。）

The pizza had the same colors as the Italian national flag.

（那時候的披薩有著與義大利國旗相同的顏色。）

The Italian national flag is red, white and green.（義大利國旗是紅色、白色和綠色。）

The pizza had red tomatoes, white cheese and green herb.

（披薩有紅色的番茄、白色的起士和綠色的香草。）

There are many different kinds of pizza today.（現今有非常多種披薩。）

We can order chicken pizza, vegetable pizza, seafood pizza, fruit pizza and so on in a pizza café or order one by making a phone call at home or in the office.

（我們能在披薩餐廳訂購雞肉披薩、蔬菜披薩、海鮮披薩、水果披薩…等，或者透過家裡或辦公室的電話來訂購。）

Some pizza has tomatoes, but some doesn't.（有些披薩有番茄有些則沒有。）

Most pizza is round, but some isn't.（大部分的披薩是圓的，但有些不是。）

You can choose any kind you want.（你可以選擇任何你想要的種類。）

People all over the world like to eat pizza.（全世界的人們喜歡吃披薩。）

How about you?（你呢？）

---

21. Pizza is very popular in the world.

（披薩在世界上非常受歡迎。）

答案：(T 對)

22. The name of the world's first pizza restaurant is Naples.

（世界上第一間披薩餐廳叫做 Naples。）

答案：（F 錯）

23. The first modern pizza was made more than 100 years ago.

（第一個現代披薩是在一百多年前製作的。）

答案：（T 對）

24. The first modern pizza looked like the Italian national flag.

（第一個現代披薩看起來像義大利國旗。）

答案：（F 錯）

25. People can only order pizza in a pizza café.

（人們在披薩餐廳只能點披薩。）

答案：（F 錯）

Ⅵ、Listen to the five questions and tick the correct boxes to complete the menu.（根據你所聽到的五個問題，在正確方框內打勾，完成 Amy 的菜單。）（5分）

Question Number 1:

Amy is in Wendy's Café now. She would like a cheap sandwich. What kind of sandwich would she like?

（問題一：Amy 現在在 Wendy's 餐廳。她想買便宜的三明治。她會喜歡哪一種三明治？）

Question Number 2:

Amy doesn't like seafood. What kind of main course would she choose?

（問題二：Amy 不喜歡海鮮。她會選擇哪一種主餐？）

Question Number 3:

Amy likes vegetables very much. So what do you think she would like to have for soup?

（問題三：Amy 非常喜歡蔬菜。你認為她會喜歡哪一種湯？）

Question Number 4:

For salad, she would like something with fruit. What kind of salad would she like?

（問題四：至於沙拉，她想要有水果的。她會喜歡哪一種沙拉？）

Question Number 5:

Amy wants a hot drink, but she doesn't like tea. What would she like to drink?

（問題五：Amy 想要熱的飲料，但是她不喜歡茶。她會喜歡喝甚麼？）

Wendy's Café（Wendy 的餐廳）

26. Sandwiches（with）三明治（附加）

☐ Chicken ￥6.50（雞肉 6.5元）

☐ Beef ¥7.50（牛肉 7.5元）

☒ Ham ¥5.00（火腿 5.00元）

27. Meat/Seafood（肉類/海鮮）

☒ Fried chicken wings ¥20.00（炸雞翅 20.00元）

☐ Steamed prawns with garlic ¥35.00（大蒜蒸明蝦 35.00元）

28. Soup（湯）

☐ Tomato and egg soup ¥6.00（番茄蛋花湯 6.00元）

☒ Tomato soup ¥5.00（番茄湯 5.00元）

☐ Cabbage soup with beef ¥10.00（牛肉高麗菜湯 10.00元）

☐ Fish soup ¥10.00（鮮魚湯 10.00元）

29. Salad（沙拉）

☐ Vegetable salad ¥5.00（蔬菜沙拉 5.00元）

☒ Fruit salad ¥5.00（水果沙拉 5.00元）

30. Drinks（飲料）

☒ Coffee ¥5.00（咖啡 5.00元）

☐ Tea ¥4.00（茶 4.00元）

☐ Apple juice ¥4.00（蘋果汁 4.00元）

全新國中會考英語聽力精選(下)原文及參考答案

Unit 9

I、Listen and choose the right picture. （根據你聽到的內容,選出相應的圖片。）（6分）

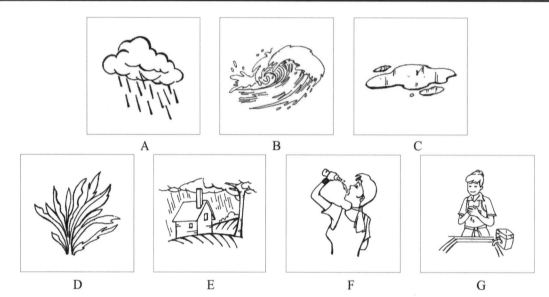

1. The big wave took away many people's lives. （大浪奪走了很多人的生命。）
   答案：(B)

2. This kind of leaves is always seen in rivers and lakes.
   （這種葉子總是可以在河川和湖泊中被看到。）
   答案：(D)

3. When we wash our hands, please don't leave the water running.
   （當我們洗手時，請不要讓水放著流。）
   答案：(G)

4. The heavy rain didn't destroy the well-built house.
   （豪雨沒有摧毀這幢蓋得很好的的房子。）
   答案：(E)

5. It is necessary to drink some water if you finish the exercise.
   （如果你運動完，喝一些水是必要的。）
   答案：(F)

6. I see water on the road. Did it rain just now?
   （我看到路上有水。剛才是不是有下雨？）
   答案：(C)

7. M: Would you like something to drink, coffee or tea?
    （男：您想喝點什麼，咖啡或是茶？）
    W: Neither. Just some water, please.（女：都不要。只要一些水，麻煩您。）
    M: OK, wait a minute.（男：好的，等一下。）
    Q: What would the girl like to drink?（問題：這位女孩想要喝什麼？）
    (A)Water.（水。）   (B)Coffee.（咖啡。）
    (C)Tea.（茶。）   (D)Wine.（葡萄酒。）
    答案：(A)

8. M: Have you paid the water bill?（男：妳付了水費帳單嗎？）
    W: Yes. This month, I used 18 litres of water and each litre costs 6 dollars.
    　（女：是的。這個月，我用了十八公升的水而每公升要六美元。）
    M: It is a large sum. Remember to save water.（男：是個大數目。記得要省水。）
    Q: How much did the lady have to pay for the water she used this month?
    　（問題：這位淑女為這個月所使用的水需要付多少錢？）
    (A)18 dollars.（十八美元。）   (B)80 dollars.（八十美元。）
    (C)480 dollars.（四百八十美元。）   (D)108 dollars.（一百零八美元。）
    答案：(D)

9. M: How do you save water at school?（男：妳在學校如何省水？）
    W: I think the best way is to remember to turn off the tap.
    　（女：我認為最好的方法是記得關掉水龍頭。）
    M: A lot of students always forget to do so. I think the most important thing is to help those
    　students to realize the importance of water.（男：一大堆學生總是忘記這樣做。我認為最
    　重要的事是幫助那些學生們領悟水的重要。）
    W: I agree with you.（女：我同意你的說法。）
    Q: What does the man suggest the girl do to save water?
    　（問題：這位男士建議這位女孩怎樣省水？）
    (A)Turn off the tap.（關掉水龍頭。）
    (B)Use less water.（用較少水。）
    (C)Educate those who waste water.（教育那些浪費水的人。）
    (D)Tell others to drink less.（叫其他人少喝一點。）
    答案：(C)

10. M: My mother is cooking now. Can you stay to have dinner with us?
    　（男：我母親正在煮飯。妳可以留下來跟我們一起吃晚餐嗎？）
    W: That's nice. But my father is sick and in bed. I have to go back to cook for him.（女：真好。

但是我父親臥病在床。我必須回去為他煮飯。）

M: Can I help?（男：我能幫忙嗎？）

W: I can manage and don't worry about me and my father.

（女：我可以搞定的，別擔心我和我父親。）

Q: What is the girl's father doing now?（問題：這位女孩的父親正在做什麼？）

(A)Seeing the doctor.（看醫生。）　　(B)Cooking.（煮飯。）

(C)Having dinner.（吃晚餐。）　　(D)Lying in bed.（躺在床上。）

答案：(D)

11. M: Jane likes watching football and her brother, Jack, enjoys playing basketball.（男：珍喜歡看足球而她兄弟傑克喜歡打籃球。）

W: I know something about them. Their parents are both famous swimmers.

（女：我知道一些關於他們的事。他們的父母都是有名的游泳健將。）

M: Your father is also a well-known tennis player. So do you like it?

（男：妳父親也是位家喻戶曉的網球選手。那麼妳喜歡網球嗎？）

W: I have no interest in it. I just want to learn the best skills of swimming from Jane's mother.

（女：我對它沒有興趣。我只想向珍的母親學最好的游泳技巧。）

Q: Which sport is Jack's father good at?（問題：傑克的父親拿手的是哪一項運動？）

(A)Basketball.（籃球）　　(B)Swimming.（游泳）

(C)Tennis.（網球）　　(D)Football.（足球）

答案：(B)

12. M: Sally, you are writing a letter on the paper, aren't you?

（男：莎麗，妳在紙上寫一封信，不是嗎？）

W: I have to. My computer has been controlled by my parents for a week.

（女：我必須這樣。我的電腦被我的父母控制一星期了。）

M: I am sorry to hear that. Go ahead.（男：我很遺憾聽到這消息。繼續吧。）

Q: Why doesn't the girl write letters on a computer but on the paper?

（問題：為何這位女孩不在電腦上而在紙上寫信？）

(A)She doesn't want to send an email.（她不想寄電子郵件。）

(B)She has been controlled by the computer.（她被電腦所控制。）

(C)Her parents asked her to write on the paper.（她父母要求她寫在紙上。）

(D)She is not allowed to use the computer.（她不被允許使用電腦。）

答案：(D)

13. M: Where are you from, Maggie?（男：妳從哪裡來的，梅姬？）

W: I lived in the UK when I was young, but I am an American.

（女：我小時候住在英國，但我是美國人。）

M: Why do you choose to work in China?（男：為何妳選擇在中國工作？）

W: The job here is attractive and I want to meet the challenge.

（女：這裡的工作很吸引人而且我想要迎接挑戰。）

Q: Where does the woman work?（問題：這位女士在哪裡工作？）

(A)In the U.K.（在英國。）   (B)In the U.S.A.（在美國。）

(C)In the P.R.C.（在中國。）   (D)In the U.N.（在聯合國。）

答案：(C)

14. M: Have you ever heard about Wolf and Goat?（男：妳可曾聽過「狼和山羊」？）

    W: It's about the interesting and funny stories between a lovely goat and a bad wolf.（女：那是關於可愛的山羊和壞狼之間有趣又好笑的故事。）

    M: It sounds not bad. What's the duration of it?（男：聽起來不賴。它有多長？）

    W: Around two hours.（女：兩小時左右。）

    Q: What are they talking about?（問題：他們在談論什麼？）

(A)A movie.（一部電影。）   (B)A book.（一本書。）

(C)A magazine.（一本雜誌。）   (D)A story.（一則故事。）

答案：(A)

15. M: What's the matter with you, Alice?（男：妳是怎麼了，愛莉絲？）

    W: I am not feeling well and have a serious stomachache.

    （女：我感覺不太舒服且有嚴重的胃痛。）

    M: Did you eat too much or anything spicy this morning?

    （男：妳今天早上有吃太飽或任何辣的東西嗎？）

    W: In fact, I had nothing for breakfast.（女：實際上，我早餐什麼都沒吃。）

    Q: What is probably the reason that the girl has a stomachache?

    （問題：這位女孩胃痛可能是什麼原因？）

(A)She ate much spicy food.（她吃太多辣的食物。）

(B)She liked eating too much.（她喜歡吃太多。）

(C)She didn't have her breakfast.（她沒吃早餐。）

(D)She was not feeling well.（她感覺不舒服。）

答案：(C)

16. M: I am sorry I am late for the charity fair, Mrs. Wang.

    （男：很抱歉慈善市集我遲到了，王太太。）

    W: Better late than never. Come on!（女：遲到總比沒到好。來吧！）

    Q: What does the woman mean?（問題：這位女士的意思是？）

(A)She wants the boy never to be late again.（她希望這位男孩再也不要遲到。）

(B)She isn't angry with the boy.（她沒有對這位男孩生氣。）

(C)She wants the boy never to come to the fair.

    （她希望這位男孩根本不要來市集。）

(D)She doesn't care about the boy.（她不在乎這位男孩。）

答案：(B)

Among national parks, Yellowstone is number one in many ways. It's the first national park in the world and it's the largest park in the United States, with a very large area.

在國家公園當中,黃石公園在很多方面都是第一名。它是全世界第一座國家公園也是美國最大的公園,占地很廣大。

Wild animals in Yellowstone are under good protection. They do not live in cages like animals in most zoos. The park is large enough for animals to walk freely like in the wild. They are able to live in a natural way. Many people have visited the park since it opened in 1872.

黃石公園裡的野生動物都受到很好的保護。牠們不像大多數動物園的動物住在籠子裡。這公園大到足以讓動物自由走動就像在野外。牠們能夠以自然的方式生活。自從它於 1872 年開放以來很多人參觀過此公園。

Many animals in the park are not afraid of people. Sometimes people can get close to them easily. But people can't hunt or feed animals in the park, because hunting or feeding will disturb animals' life.

此公園裡很多動物不害怕人。有時候人們可以輕易地靠近牠們。但是人們不能在公園內獵捕或餵食動物,因為打獵或餵食會打擾到動物的生活。

Yellowstone National Park sets a good example of how people and wild animals live together peacefully. Putting animals in cages is not a good way to protect them. If people realize the importance of wild animals, they should give animals a comfortable living environment.

黃石國家公園為人類和野生動物如何一起和平生活樹立了一個好的典範。把動物放在籠子裡不是保護牠們的好方法。如果人們了解野生動物的重要性,他們應該給予動物們一個舒適的生活環境。

17. Yellowstone is the first park in America and even in the world.
（黃石公園是美國,甚至是全世界的第一座公園。）
答案：(F 錯)

18. Yellowstone has been open for more than 130 years.
（黃石公園開放已經超過一百三十年。）
答案：(T 對)

19. There are no cages in Yellowstone, but animals are unable to live in a natural way.（在黃石公園裡沒有籠子,但是動物們不能以自然的方式生活。）
答案：(F 錯)

20. Animals in Yellowstone are quite happy if people feed food to them.
（黃石公園裡的動物會頗開心如果人們餵牠們食物。）

答案：(F 錯)

21. Hunting animals in Yellowstone will bring damage to animals' life.
（在黃石公園裡獵捕動物會對動物的生活帶來災害。）
答案：(T 對)

22. People and wild animals live together peacefully in Yellowstone.
（在黃石公園裡人類和野生動物在一起和平地生活。）
答案：(T 對)

23. In most zoos, animals are kept in cages. （在大多數動物園裡，動物被養在籠子裡。）
答案：(T 對)

IV、Listen to the passage and fill in the blanks with proper words. （聽短文,用最恰當的詞填空,每格限填一詞）（共 7 分）

Rivers are one of our most important natural resources. Many of the world's great cities are located on rivers, and almost every country has at least one river flowing through it that plays an important part in the life of its people.

河川是我們最重要的自然資源之一。世界上很多大都市都位於河川上，幾乎每個國家都有至少一條河川流經，並且在國民的生活中扮演著重要的角色。

Since the beginning of history, people have used rivers for transportation. The longest one in the United States is the Mississippi. The lifeline of Egypt is the Nile, and it is also important for transportation. Ships can travel along it for a thousand miles. Other great rivers are the Congo in Africa and the Mekong in Southeast Asia. The greatest of all for navigation, however, is the Amazon in Brazil. It is so wide and so deep that large ships can go about thousands of miles upon it.

從歷史的開端，人們就利用河川來運輸。美國最長的一條是密西西比河。埃及的生命線是尼羅河，它也因運輸而有其重要性。船隻可以沿著它運行一千英里。其它偉大的河川是非洲的剛果河和東南亞的湄公河。然而，航行上最了不起的是巴西的亞馬遜河。它那麼寬又那麼深所以大船可以在上面航行大約數千英里。

Besides transportation, rivers give food, water to drink, water to irrigate fields, and chances for fun and recreation for the people who live along their banks. However, large cities and industries that are located upon rivers often cause problems. As the cities grow in size and industries increase in number, the water in the rivers becomes polluted with chemicals and other materials. People are realizing the importance of doing more to keep their rivers clean if they want to enjoy the benefits of this natural resource.

運輸之外，河川提供住在它沿岸的人們食物、飲用水、灌溉田園用水和娛樂及休閒的可能性。然而，位於河川上的大都市和工業常常造成問題。隨著都市規模成長和工業數量增加，河川中的水變成被化學藥劑和其他物質所汙染。人們正領悟到多努力維持他們的河川乾淨的重要性，如果他們想要享受這自然資源的好處。

- Rivers, as a kind of __24__ resources, are quite important.
  （河川，因為是一種自然資源，所以頗重要。）
- At least one river __25__ through a country and it plays an important role.
  （至少一條河流經一個國家且它扮演一個重要的角色。）
- The Nile is the longest river worldwide and is the lifeline of __26__.
  （尼羅河是全世界最長的河，且是埃及的生命線。）
- Large ships can go about thousands of miles upon the Amazon because it is so __27__ and wide.
  （大船可在亞馬遜河上航行約數千英里因為它那麼深又寬。）
- Rivers also give food, water to drink, water to irrigate __28__, and chances for fun. （河川也提供食物、飲用水、灌溉田園用水和娛樂的機會。）
- The problem of river pollution is __29__ by chemicals and other materials from large cities or industries located upon rivers.
  （河川污染的問題是來自河川上的大都市或工業的化學藥劑和其他物質所造成。）
- Keeping rivers clean can make human beings enjoy the __30__ of this natural resource.
  （維持河川乾淨可使人類享受這個自然資源的好處。）

24. 答案：natural 自然
25. 答案：flows 流
26. 答案：Egypt 埃及
27. 答案：deep 深
28. 答案：fields 田園
29. 答案：caused 造成
30. 答案：benefits 好處

Unit 10

I 、Listen and choose the right picture.（根據你所聽到的內容，選出相應的圖片。）（6分）

A.   B.   C.

D.   E.   F.   G.

1. Ben is playing chess with Jack in the sitting room. Where are the other children?
   （Ben 跟 Jack 在起居室下西洋棋。其他孩子在哪裡？）

   答案：(C)

2. Shall we sing karaoke after the meeting?
   （我們會議之後去唱卡拉 OK 好嗎？）

   答案：(E)

3. Alice and her brother always spend much time watching TV at weekends.
   （Alice 和她哥哥總是在周末花很多時間看電視。）

   答案：(B)

4. Let's have a barbecue party. It will be very interesting.
   （我們來辦個烤肉宴會吧。那一定很有趣。）

   答案：(A)

5. Make a wish, Ben. (Sing) Happy birthday to you, happy birthday to you ...
    （Ben，許個願。(唱歌)祝你生日快樂，祝你生日快樂……）
    答案：

6. Mum, are the cakes ready? We are hungry.
    （媽，蛋糕準備好了嗎？我們餓了。）
    答案：(F)

II、Listen and choose the best response to the sentence you hear.（根據你所聽到的句子，選出最恰當的應答句。）(6分)

7. May I speak to Ben, please?
    （請找 Ben 聽電話。）
    (A)Who are you?（你是誰？）
    (B)This is Ben speaking.（我是 Ben。）
    (C)Is that Ben?（那是 Ben 嗎？）
    (D)Are you Ben speaking?（你是 Ben 在說話嗎？）
    答案：(B)

8. For Ben's birthday party, we're going to have a barbecue in the evening.
    （為了 Ben 的生日宴會，我們將在晚上烤肉。）
    (A)Whose idea?（誰的點子？）
    (B)Sounds terrible!（聽起來太可怕了！）
    (C)That sounds great.（聽起來很棒。）
    (D)I won't go with you.（我不會跟你去。）
    答案：(C)

9. I'll see you on Saturday afternoon at three o'clock at my flat.
    （我星期天下午三點在我家跟你碰面。）
    (A)See you then.（那時候見。）
    (B)I have no time.（我沒時間。）
    (C)I will go by myself.（我會自己去。）
    (D)Thank you very much.（非常感謝你。）
    答案：(A)

10. I'm sorry that I have something important to do this Saturday. I can't go to Ben's birthday party.
（這個星期天我有重要的事要做，真抱歉。我不能去 Ben 的生日宴會。）

(A)Oh, it sounds great. （喔，聽起來真棒。）

(B)Have a great dream. （祝你有個好夢。）

(C)Have a good time. （祝你有個愉快的時光。）

(D)Oh, what a pity! （喔，好可惜！）

答案：(D)

11. What ingredients do we need to make a chocolate cake?
（做巧克力蛋糕我們需要甚麼材料？）

(A)We need some eggs, some sugar, some butter, some flour and some chocolate powder.
（我們需要蛋、糖、奶油、麵粉和巧克力粉。）

(B)We have to go to the supermarket to buy these things.
（我們要去超級市場買那些東西。）

(C)We need to buy some eggs, some flour and some chocolate powder first.
（我們需要先買蛋、麵粉和巧克力粉。）

(D)Can you show me how to bake a chocolate cake?
（你能教我怎麼做巧克力蛋糕嗎？）

答案：(A)

12. What food shall we have at the party?
（宴會上我們需要甚麼食物呢？）

(A)No. We don't need any food. （不。我們不需要任何食物。）

(B)Let's have some spicy sausages! （讓我們來些辣香腸吧。）

(C)Are there any soft drinks? （有碳酸飲料嗎？）

(D)I can't agree with you. （我不同意你。）

答案：(B)

Ⅲ、Listen to the dialogue and choose the best answer to the question you hear. （根據你所聽到的對話和問題，選出最恰當的答案。）（6分）

---

13. W: It's John's birthday tomorrow. Are you coming, Eddie?
（W: 明天是 John 的生日。Eddie, 你要來嗎？）

M: Yes, of course. I have a surprise present for him.
（M: 當然要。我有一個驚喜的禮物要給他。）

W: What is it?

（W: 那是甚麼？）

Question: What is true according to the dialogue?
（問題：根據這段對話，甚麼是真的？）

(A)Tomorrow is Eddie's birthday.
（明天是 Eddie 的生日。）

(B)There is going to be a surprise birthday party.
（將會有一場驚喜的生日宴會）

(C)Eddie won't go to the birthday party.
（Eddie 不去生日宴會。）

(D)John will have a surprise birthday present from Eddie.
（John 將會有一個 Eddie 給的驚喜生日禮物。）

答案：(D)

14. W: What present have you got for John, Eddie?
　　（W: Eddie，你要給 John 甚麼禮物？）

M: A puppy. John likes dogs very much. What about you, Sandra?
　　（M: 一隻小狗。John 非常喜歡狗。Sandra，你呢？）

W: Don't you know he likes hot dogs better?
　　（W: 你不知道他更喜歡熱狗嗎？）

Question: What can you learn from the dialogue?
　　（問題：從這段對話你可以知道甚麼？）

(A)John doesn't like hot dogs.（John 不喜歡熱狗。）

(B)John likes dogs.（John 喜歡狗。）

(C)Sandra will give John a puppy.（Sandra 要給 John 一隻小狗。）

(D)Eddie will give John a hot dog.（Eddie 要給 John 一個熱狗。）

答案：(B)

15. W: What food shall we have at the party?
　　（W: 我們在宴會應該有甚麼食物呢？）

M: Let's have some fried chicken wings.
　　（M: 讓我們準備一些炸雞翅吧。）

W: I don't like fried food.
　　（W: 我不喜歡煎炸的食物。）

Question: What food will the girl prefer?
　　（問題：那個女孩比較喜歡甚麼食物？）

(A)Fried fish finger.（炸魚條。）

(B)Fried rice.（炒飯。）

(C)Chicken.（雞肉。）

(D)KFC.（肯德基。）

答案：(C)

16. W: What are you doing here, Eddie?

（W: Eddie，你在這裡做甚麼？）

M: Mum asks me to buy some ingredients for the cake.

（M: 媽要我去為蛋糕買一些材料。）

W: What will you buy?

（W: 你要買甚麼？）

M: Mm, some sugar, some flour, some eggs, some chocolate and some butter.

（M: 嗯，糖、麵粉、蛋、巧克力和奶油。）

Question: What ingredient is not needed in Mum's cake?

（問題：媽媽的蛋糕裡不需要的材料是甚麼？）

(A)Sugar.（糖。）

(B)Icing sugar.（冰糖。）

(C)Chocolate.（巧克力。）

(D)Eggs.（蛋。）

答案：(B)

17. W: Would you like to have a look at my photos?

（W: 你想看看我的照片嗎？）

M: Who's that funny man?

（W: 那個有趣的男人是誰？）

W: Oh, he's my brother. He dressed up as Mickey at my party.

（W: 喔，他是我弟弟。他在我的宴會上打扮成 Mickey。）

Question: When does this dialogue take place?

（問題：這段對話何時發生的呢？）

(A)At the party.（在宴會上。）

(B)Before the party.（在宴會之前。）

(C)After the party.（在宴會之後。）

(D)We don't know.（我們不知道。）

答案：(C)

18. M: Ben told us to go to his birthday party at 7 o'clock. Right?

（M: Ben 告訴我們七點去他的生日宴會。對嗎？）

W: Yes. It's twenty to seven by my watch now.

（W: 對。我的手錶現在是六點四十分。）

M: Don't worry. We still have enough time. Your watch is fifteen minutes fast.
  （M: 別擔心。我們還有足夠的時間。你的錶快了十五分鐘。）

W: Oh ...
  （W: 喔...）

Question: What time is it now?
  （問題：現在幾點？）

(A)6.25.（六點二十五分。）

(B)6.40.（六點四十分。）

(C)6.55.（六點五十五分。）

(D)7.00.（七點。）

答案：(A)

IV、Listen to the dialogue and decide whether the following statements are True (T) or False (F).（判斷下列句子內容是否符合你所聽到的對話內容，符合的用"T"表示，不符合的用"F"表示。）（6分）

W: Can I have a look at your photos?
（W: 我可以看看你的照片嗎？）

M: Yes, of course. Here you are.
（M:當然可以。在這裡。）

W: Is it you, Tommy?
（W: Tommy，這是你嗎？）

M: Yes. I was ten years old that day. You can read the captions on the back of the photos.
（M: 是。那天我十歲。你可以看照片背後的說明。）

W: I see. You sang Karaoke with your friends.
（W: 我知道了。你跟你朋友一起唱卡拉 OK。）

M: We also had a barbecue next.
（M: 我們接下來還有烤肉。）

W: What a big cake!
（W: 好大的蛋糕喔！）

M: My mum made it for my birthday.
（M: 我媽媽為我的生日而做的。）

W: You had a great day, Tommy.
（W: Tommy，你玩得很開心。）

---

19. It was Tommy's eleventh birthday party.

（那是 Tommy 的十一歲生日宴會。）

答案：（F 錯）

20. There were no captions on the back of the photos.
（照片背後沒有說明。）

答案：（F 錯）

21. They sang karaoke that day.
（他們那天唱卡拉 OK。）

答案：（T 對）

22. They watched some cartoons.
（他們看了一些卡通。）

答案：（F 錯）

23. They had a cake made by Tommy's mother.
（他們有一個 Tommy 的母親做的蛋糕。）

答案：（T 對）

24. Tommy and his friends had a good time that day.
（Tommy 和他的朋友那天玩得很開心。）

答案：（T 對）

Ⅴ、Listen and fill in the blanks.（根據你所聽到的內容，用適當的單詞完成下面的句子。每空格限填一詞。）（6分）

Pizza is a kind of popular food.
（披薩是一種受歡迎的食物。）
It has a long history.
（它有悠久的歷史。）
Most people think it comes from Italy.
（大部分的人認為它來自義大利。）
The world's first pizza restaurant is in Naples, a famous city in Italy.
（世界上最早的一間披薩餐廳是在那不勒斯，一個有名的義大利城市。）
It opened more than 100 years ago.
（它在一百多年前開張。）
Modern pizza was first made by a person named Refael Esposito in the 1880s.
（現代披薩在 1880 年代第一次由一個叫做 Refael Esposito 的人做出來的。）
The pizza had the same colors as the Italian national flag.

（披薩有著與義大利國旗一樣的顏色。）

The Italian national flag is red, white and green.

（義大利國旗是紅色、白色和綠色。）

The pizza had red tomatoes, white cheese and green herb.

（披薩有紅色的番茄、白色的起士，和綠色的香草。）

There are many different kinds of pizza today.

（現今有非常多種披薩。）

We can order chicken pizza, vegetable pizza, seafood pizza, fruit pizza and so on in a pizza café or order one by making a phone call at home or in the office.

（我們可以在披薩餐廳點雞肉披薩、蔬菜披薩、海鮮披薩、水果披薩等等，或者可以透過家裡或辦公室的電話訂購。）

Some pizza has tomatoes, but some doesn't.

（有些披薩有番茄，有些則沒有。）

Most pizza is round, but some isn't.

（大部分的披薩是圓的，但有些不是。）

You can choose any kind you want.

（你可以選擇任何一種你想要的。）

People all over the world like to eat pizza.

（全世界的人們喜歡吃披薩。）

How about you?

（你呢？）

- The world's first pizza __25__ is in Naples, a famous city in Italy.
  （世界上第一個披薩是在義大利一個有名的城市，那不勒斯，的＿＿＿。）

- The pizza had the same colors as the Italian national __26__.
  （披薩有著與義大利國＿＿＿相同的顏色。）

- The pizza had red __27__, white cheese and green herb.
  （披薩有紅色的＿＿＿，白色的起士和綠色的香草。）

- We can order chicken pizza, vegetable pizza, seafood pizza or __28__ pizza in a pizza café.
  （我們可以在披薩餐廳點雞肉披薩、蔬菜披薩、海鮮披薩或＿＿＿披薩。）

- We can also order a pizza by making a phone call at home or in the __29__.
  （我們也可以透過家裡或＿＿＿的電話訂購披薩。）

- People can choose any __30__ they want.
  （人們可以選擇任何＿＿＿他們想要的。）

25. 答案：restaurant (餐廳)

26. 答案：flag (旗子)

27. 答案：tomatoes (番茄)

28. 答案：fruit (水果)

29. 答案：office (辦公室)

30. 答案：kind (種類)

Unit 11

I 、Listen and choose the right picture. (根據你聽到的內容,選出相應的圖片。) (6分)

1. Mrs. Wang is reading a story from the book to her children.
   （王太太正在給她的孩子們唸書上的一則故事。）
   答案：(D)

2. Danny is busy doing his homework and he is hard working.
   （丹尼正忙著做他的作業，他很用功。）
   答案：(F)

3. The naughty boy has grown up and he works as a pilot.
   （這頑皮的男孩已經長大做了飛行員的工作。）
   答案：(A)

4. A little girl is dancing around a tree as the tree was planted by her last year.
   （一位小女孩正繞著一棵樹跳舞，因為這樹就是她去年種下的。）
   答案：(B)

5. Daisy is thinking about why fish live in water.
   （黛西正想著為什麼魚兒在水中生活。）
   答案：(G)

6. Danny is walking freely on a sunny day. （丹尼在一個晴朗的日子自由地漫步著。）
   答案：(C)

7. W: Do you like reading newspapers or magazines?（女：你喜歡看報紙或是雜誌？）

    M: I am a football fan, so my favorite is the monthly football magazine called Football Family.

    （男：我是個足球迷，所以我的最愛是名為足球家族的足球雜誌月刊。）

    Q: How often is the magazine the man likes published?

    （問題：這位男士所喜歡的雜誌的出版頻率是？）

    (A)Every day.每天。）   (B)Once a week.一星期一次。）

    (C)Twice a month.每月兩次。）   (D)Every month. 每個月。）

    答案：(D)

8. W: Don't waste time on these newspapers. Please finish your homework as soon as possible.

    （女：別把時間浪費在這些報紙上。請盡速完成你的作業。）

    M: It's what my teacher asked me to do. I am looking for what I want.

    （男：這是我的老師要求我做的。我正在找我要的。）

    Q: Why does the boy spend time on the newspapers?

    （問題：為何這位男孩花時間在報紙上？）

    (A)Because his teacher wanted to borrow the newspapers.

    （因為他的老師想要借報紙。）

    (B)Because reading newspapers is his favorite activity.

    （因為閱讀報紙是他最喜歡的活動。）

    (C)Because it is his homework.（因為這是他的作業。）

    (D)Because he is looking for someone he wants to meet.

    （因為他在尋找他想要見的某個人。）

    答案：(C)

9. W: When should the postman send China Daily to my box?

    （女：郵差應該什麼時間把中國日報送到我的信箱？）

    M: Regularly at 3 p.m.（男：固定在下午三點。）

    W: But today he was half an hour late.（女：但是今天他晚了半小時。）

    M: On rainy days, postmen come a little bit late as they have to prepare some coverings.（男：

    在下雨天郵差會晚一點來，因為他們必須準備一些遮蓋物。）

    Q: When did the woman receive her newspaper today?

    （問題：這位女士今天幾點收到她的報紙？）

    (A)At 3:30.   (B)At 4:00.   (C)At 3:00.   (D)She didn't get the

    newspaper.她沒有收到報紙。

    答案：(A)

10. W: Would you mind passing me that magazine?

（女：你介意把那本雜誌遞給我嗎？）

M: Sure. By the way, how long have you stayed here reading?

（男：沒問題。對了，妳待在這裡閱讀了多久？）

W: All morning. It is quiet here and I enjoy the environment.

（女：整個上午。這裡很安靜且我喜歡這環境。）

Q: Where does this dialogue take place?（問題：這段會話在哪裡發生？）

(A)At a drug store.在一間藥店。）

(B)In the boy's home.在這位男孩的家中。）

(C)In a reading room.在一間閱讀室。）

(D)In a dining room.在飯廳。）

答案：(C)

11. W: Anything new?（女：有什麼新鮮事？）

M: It says on the front page that some Hong Kong people were killed by a policeman on a bus.

（男：在頭版說有些香港人被一位警察在一輛巴士上殺害了。）

W: Oh, my god. Some good news for me?

（女：噢，我的天。可以給我一些好消息嗎？）

M: The forecast says that tomorrow a fierce typhoon will come and we won't go to school.

（男：天氣預報說明天有一個強烈的颱風要來，我們不用去學校。）

Q: What is the boy doing now?（問題：這位男孩現在正在做什麼？）

(A)Watching TV.（看電視。）

(B)Reading a newspaper.（看報紙。）

(C)Listening to the radio.（聽收音機。）

(D)Chatting on the Internet.（在網路上聊天。）

答案：(B)

12. W: What's the matter with you?（女：你是怎麼了？）

M: I have a sore throat. What should I do then?（男：我喉嚨痛。那我該怎麼辦？）

W: Speak less. Having a rest is always more useful than medicine.

（女：少說話。休息一下總是比藥更有用。）

Q: What does the woman suggest the man do to treat his sore throat?

（問題：這位女士建議這位男士做什麼以治療他的喉嚨痛？）

(A)Take some medicine.（吃些藥。）　　　(B)Have a break.（休息一下。）

(C)Speak more.（多說話。）　　　　　　(D)Go to the doctor's.（去看醫生。）

答案：(B)

13. W: I think I can win the game and nobody else can beat me.

（女：我想我可以贏這個比賽且沒人可以打敗我。）

M: It is easier said than done.（男：說比做容易。）

Q: What can we learn from the man?（問題：從這位男士我們可以得知？）

(A)The man agrees with the woman.（這位男士同意這位女士所說。）

(B)The man thinks it is impossible for the woman to win.

（這位男士認為這位女士不可能贏。）

(C)The man disagrees with the woman.（這位男士不同意這位女士所說。）

(D)The man thinks actions speak louder than words.

（這位男士認為事實勝於雄辯。）

答案：(D)

14. W: Have you ever seen a red pen? I left it on the desk.

（女：你有看到過一隻紅筆嗎？我把它留在書桌上。）

M: Is it a wooden one? I saw it on the shelf just now.

（男：是木頭的嗎？我剛剛才在架子上看到它。）

W: That's it. Can you put it in my pencil-box?

（女：就是它。你可以把它放到我的鉛筆盒裡嗎？）

M: OK, I will go and take it back.（男：好的，我會去把它拿回來。）

Q: Where did the girl leave the red pen?（問題：這位女孩把紅筆留在哪裡？）

(A)In the pencil-box.（在鉛筆盒裡。）　　　　(B)On the shelf.（在架子上。）

(C)On the desk.（在書桌上。）　　　　　　　(D)In a wooden box.（在一個木盒子裡。）

答案：(C)

15. W: Would you like to have the flat with two bathrooms?

（女：你會想要有兩間浴室的公寓嗎？）

M: It will be more convenient. Is there a study in the flat?

（男：那樣會比較方便。在那間公寓裡有書房嗎？）

W: The balcony of the flat is big enough for you to leave space for study.

（女：這間公寓的陽台夠大到讓你留下空間來讀書。）

Q: What does the flat have?　（問題：這間公寓有什麼？）

(A)A big balcony.（一個大陽台。）　　　　(B)A study.（一間書房。）

(C)Three bathrooms.（三間浴室。）　　　　(D)A small bathroom.（一間小臥室。）

答案：(A)

16. W: Sandy is a model student in our class and she likes writing diaries.

（女：珊蒂是我們班上的模範學生，她喜歡寫日記。）

M: How do you know that? I know Sandy does well in English.

（男：妳怎麼知道的？我知道珊蒂在英文上表現很好。）

W: Yes. Last time, she sang a lot of English songs for us and her voice was wonderful.（女：是的。上一次，她為我們唱了很多英文歌，她的聲音很棒。）

Q: Which statement can't be used to describe Sandy?

（問題：何敘述不能用來形容珊蒂？）

(A)She is good at English.（她對英文很拿手。）

(B)She likes writing diaries.（她喜歡寫日記。）

(C)She enjoys writing songs.（她喜愛寫歌曲。）

(D)She sings English songs well.（她英文歌唱得好。）

答案：(C)

Ⅲ、Listen to the passage and tell whether the following statements are true or false.
（判斷下列句子是否符合你聽到的短文內容,符合用 T 表示,不符合用 F 表示）（7分）

Bill was fourteen years old and in the ninth grade. He had a part-time job and he had to get up at five o'clock. He was a newspaper boy.

比爾十四歲，九年級。他有個兼職工作，他必須五點起床。他是個報童。

Each morning Bill left the house at five fifteen to go to the corner. The newspapers had been sent to the corner by a truck at midnight. He always rode a bike to take them.

每天早上比爾在五點十五分離家前往街角。報紙已在午夜時被一輛貨車送到街角。他總是騎腳踏車去拿。

In winter it was still dark when he got up, but during the rest of the year it was bright. Bill had to send the newspapers to people's houses in all kinds of weather. He tried to put each paper in the box where it would be kept safe from wind, rain or snow. His customers thought he did a good job. Sometimes they gave him tips.

在冬天他起床的時候天仍然是黑的，但在一年當中其他時候已經天亮。比爾必須在各種天氣之下把報紙送到家家戶戶。他試著把每份報紙放到信箱以在風雨或雪中保持安全。他的客戶認為他做得很好。有時候他們給他小費。

Bill made about ＄70 each month, and he had to save most of the money to go to college. He spent the rest on tapes and clothes. Once a month he had to get the money from his customers together. Since many of them worked during the day, Bill's father had to help him.

比爾每個月賺大約七十美元，他必須存下大部分的錢好上大學。他把剩餘的錢花在錄音帶和衣服上面。每個月一次他必須向他的客戶們一起收錢。由於他們當中很多人在白天工作，比爾的父親必須幫助他。

Bill had 70 customers, but he hoped to have more. If he got more customers, perhaps he could win a prize for being a very good newspaper boy. He wanted to win a visit to Europe, but he would be happy if he won a new bike.

比爾有七十位客戶，但他希望有更多。如果他有更多客戶，或許他能夠以成為很好的報童而得到一個獎。他想要贏得一次歐洲旅遊，但如果他贏得一台新的腳踏車他也會很高興。

---

17. Bill studied in Grade Nine and had to go to school very early.

（比爾就讀九年級，必須每天很早去學校。）

答案：(F 錯)

18. Newspapers are sent to the corner at midnight by truck.
（報紙在午夜時被卡車送到街角。）
答案：(T 對)

19. Bill's customers were pleased with Bill's job.
（比爾的客戶對比爾的工作感到滿意。）
答案：(T 對)

20. Bill saved all the money he earned as a newspaper boy for college expenses.
（比爾存下全部他當報童所賺的錢以作為大學費用。）
答案：(F 錯)

21. Sometimes Bill's father helped him send newspapers to people.
（有時候比爾的父親幫助他送報紙給人們。）
答案：(F 錯)

22. Bill was a boy who might enjoy listening to music.
（比爾可能是個喜愛聽音樂的男孩。）
答案：(T 對)

23. If Bill won a new bike instead of a trip to Europe, he would feel disappointed.
（如果比爾贏得一台新的腳踏車而不是歐洲旅遊，他會感到失望。）
答案：(F 錯)

IV、Listen to the passage and fill in the blanks with proper words.（聽短文,用最恰當的詞填空,每格限填一詞）（共7分）

A newspaper reporter's job can be very exciting. He meets different types of people and lives quite a busy life. He is looking for news all the time, and after some years he may get a desk job. Sometimes he may be so busy that he has no time to sleep well. And at other times, he may go on for days looking for news material.

報紙記者的工作可以是很刺激的。他遇到不同類型的人們並且過著頗為忙碌的生活。他隨時都在尋找新聞，幾年之後他可能得到一個辦公室的工作。有時候他可能忙碌到沒時間好好睡覺。而在其他時間，他可能持續數日尋找新聞的材料。

In the beginning, a reporter has to cover a very wide area. After the early years he becomes more specialized in his work. Some reporters may become so specialized that they are asked only to write in a special area. Some newspapers have book reviews. A reporter may read the latest books and then write reviews on the ones he likes. There are those who write on films, and they can see the films even before they are shown in the cinema.

在開始的時候，一名記者必須涵蓋很廣的範圍。初期的幾年後他變得在他的工作上更專精。有些記者可能變成專精到被要求只寫一個特殊領域以內的東西。有些報紙有書籍評論。記者可能閱讀最新的書籍然後對他所喜歡的寫下評論。也有人寫關於電影的，他們甚至可以在戲院上映之前看電影。

A reporter's job can also be very dangerous. If there is a war, they may get hurt or even be killed. Three years ago there was a reporter whose camera was broken by a group of men, because they were angry with him for taking pictures of them. Dangerous or not, one thing is certain — a reporter's job is never uninteresting!

記者的工作也可以是很危險的。如果有戰爭，他們可能受傷或甚至喪生。三前年有一位記者的相機被一群人弄壞，因為他拍他們的照片使他們生氣。無論是否危險，有一件事是肯定的 — 記者的工作絕對不會無趣！

- A newspaper reporter will __24__ different kinds of people in the job.
  （報紙記者在工作上會遇到不同種類的人們。）
- A reporter may have a __25__ job after looking for news everywhere for some years. （記者在到處找尋新聞數年之後可能有辦公室的工作。）
- A reporter's job ranges from covering a __26__ area to a special one.
  （記者的工作從涵蓋廣大範圍到專精特殊領域有很多種類。）
- A reporter writes book reviews after reading the __27__ books.
  （記者在閱讀最新的書之後寫書籍評論。）
- A reporter always watches movies __28__ movies are on at cinemas.
  （記者總是在戲院上映之前看電影。）
- A group of tough guys __29__ a reporter's camera when they were taken pictures of 3 years ago.
  （三年前當一群頑強的傢伙們被拍照時弄壞了一名記者的相機。）
- A reporter's job is both exciting and dangerous but never ever __30__.
  （記者的工作是既刺激又危險，但是絕對不會無趣。）

24. 答案：meet（遇到）
25. 答案：desk（書桌）
26. 答案：wide（廣大）
27. 答案：latest（最新）
28. 答案：before（之前）
29. 答案：broke（弄壞）
30. 答案：uninteresting（無趣）

Unit 12

I、Listen and choose the right picture.（根據你所聽到的內容，選出相應的圖片。）（6分）

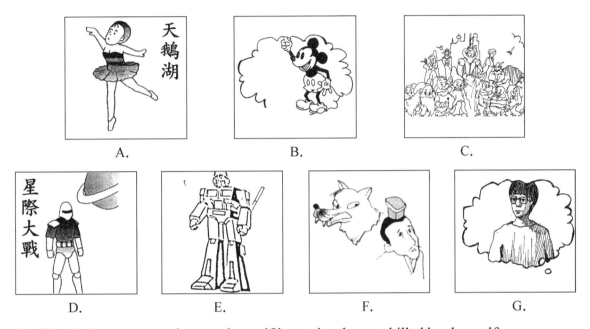

A.　　　　　　　B.　　　　　　　C.

D.　　　　　　　E.　　　　　　　F.　　　　　　　G.

1. The film is about a man who saved a wolf but at last he was killed by the wolf.
   （這是一部關於一個男人救了一匹狼但最後卻被那匹狼殺害的電影。）
   答案：(F)

2. The boy is a wizard. When he says a rhyme, he will make you stick on the wall.
   （那個男孩是個巫師。當他說了一句咒語，他就會讓你黏在牆上。）
   答案：(G)

3. I like Mickey Mouse very much.
   （我非常喜歡米老鼠。）
   答案：(B)

4. This week I will go to see the film Snow White and the Seven Dwarfs.
   （這個星期我要去看白雪公主與七個小矮人這部電影。）
   答案：(C)

5. If you are interested in ballet and love stories, you'd better go to see Swan Lake.
   （如果你對芭蕾和愛情故事感興趣，你最好去看天鵝湖。）
   答案：(A)

6. The story is about two groups of robots fighting against each other. They can change into cars or

planes.

（這個是關於兩組機器人相互對抗的故事。他們可以變成車或是飛機。）

答案：(E)

II、Listen and choose the best response to the sentence you hear.（根據你所聽到的句子，選出最恰當的應答句。）（6分）

---

7. What is the film about?

（這部電影與甚麼有關？）

(A)I don't like it.（我不喜歡它。）

(B)It's about a swan princess and a prince.（它與天鵝公主與王子有關。）

(C)It's a love story.（它是個愛情故事。）

(D)It's very exciting.（那非常刺激。）

答案：(B)

8. I don't like adventure films.

（我不喜歡冒險電影。）

(A)That's interesting.（那很有趣。）

(B)They like adventures.（他們喜歡冒險。）

(C)So do I.（我也喜歡。）

(D)Neither do I.（我也不喜歡。）

答案：(D)

9. Shall we see the film Country Road?

（我們看電影 Country Road 好嗎？）

(A)OK. Let's see Swan Lake.

（好。我們看天鵝湖吧。）

(B)I'm afraid I don't like stories about cowboys.

（我怕我不喜歡牛仔的故事。）

(C)It's a great cartoon.

（那是一部很棒的卡通。）

(D)No, that's too bad.

（不，那太糟了。）

答案：(B)

10. How can I get to the nearest McDonald's?

（我該怎麼去最近的麥當勞？）

(A)Sorry, I'm new here.（抱歉，我剛來這裡。）

(B)Yes, I can.（是的，我可以。）

(C)No, you can't.（不，你不能。）

(D)You'll find the cinema on your right.（你會在右邊看到一間電影院。）

答案：(A)

11. This cartoon is wonderful.

（這部卡通很棒。）

(A)I like watching cartoons.（我喜歡看卡通）

(B)The cartoon is on Channel 4.（卡通在四號頻道）

(C)We usually watch cartoons at weekends.（我們通常在周末看卡通。）

(D)Yes, but the music is too noisy.（是的，但是音樂太吵了。）

答案：(D)

12. I'm sorry I have left your book at home.

（很抱歉我把你的書留在家裡了。）

(A)That's all right.（沒關係。）

(B)I won't.（我不會。）

(C)All right.（好的。）

(D)Thank you.（謝謝你。）

答案：(A)

Ⅲ、Listen to the dialogue and choose the best answer to the question you hear.（根據你所聽到的對話和問題，選出最恰當的答案。）（6分）

13. W: Do you like sports, Jim?

（W: Jim，你喜歡運動嗎？）

M: Of course I do. Football, tennis, volleyball ... I like all of them. But the sport I like most is swimming.

（M: 我當然喜歡。足球、網球、排球...我都喜歡。但是我最喜歡的運動是游泳。）

Question: What sport does Jim like best?

（問題：Jim 最喜歡甚麼運動？）

(A)Swimming.（游泳。）

(B)Tennis.（網球。）

(C)Volleyball.（排球。）

(D)Football.（足球。）

答案：(A)

14. W: Are you feeling better today, Peter?

（W: Peter，你今天覺得好一點嗎？）

M: No, not really. I have a bad headache, and I can't get any sleep at night.
（M: 不，不是太好。我頭很痛，而且我昨晚沒睡。）

W: Don't worry. You'll be better soon. The doctors here are the best in the city.
（W: 別擔心。你很快就好了。這裡的醫生是城裡最好的。）

Question: Where are they talking now?
（問題：他們現在在哪裡說話？）

(A)In the bedroom.（臥室。）

(B)At school.（學校。）

(C)In the hospital.（醫院。）

(D)At a cinema.（電影院。）

答案：(C)

15. W: My family went to Century Park last Sunday.
（W: 上星期天我們全家去中央公園。）

M: Oh, great! Did you go there by car?
（M: 喔，太棒了！你們搭車去那裡嗎？）

W: Sometimes we go by car, but last Sunday we didn't.
（W: 有時候我們搭車，但是上星期天我們沒有。）

M: Did you go by bus?
（M: 你們搭公車去嗎？）

W: No, Mum doesn't like the bus. We took the underground.
（W: 不，老媽不喜歡公車。我們搭地鐵。）

Question: How did they go to the park last Sunday?
（問題：他們上星期天如何去公園？）

(A)By taxi.（搭計程車。）

(B)By car.（搭車。）

(C)By bus.（搭公車。）

(D)By underground.（搭地鐵。）

答案：(D)

16. W: What kind of film do you like best?
（W: 你最喜歡哪一種電影？）

M: Action films.
（M: 動作片。）

W: Don't you like love stories?
（W: 你不喜歡愛情故事嗎？）

M: No.

　　（M: 不喜歡。）

W: But I like love stories.

　　（W: 但是我喜歡愛情故事。）

Question: What kind of film does the woman like?

　　（問題：那個女人喜歡哪一種電影？）

(A)Action films.（動作片。）

(B)Love stories.（愛情故事。）

(C)Funny films.（趣味片。）

(D)Cartoons.（卡通。）

答案：(B)

17. M: The weather today is rather wet, isn't it?

　　　（M: 今天天氣滿潮濕的，不是嗎？）

W: Yes, but the radio says tomorrow will be a sunny day.

　　　（W: 是的，但是收音機說明天就會是晴天了。）

Question: What's the weather like today?

　　　（問題：今天天氣如何？）

(A)It's fine.（天氣很好。）

(B)It's raining.（雨天。）

(C)It's cloudy.（陰天。）

(D)It's windy.（有風。）

答案：(B)

18. M: How can I get to the zoo? Shall I take bus No. 22?

　　　（M: 我怎麼去動物園？我搭二十二號公車對嗎？）

W: No, you should take bus No. 12. There's a bus stop just over there.

　　　（W: 不，你應該搭十二號公車。那裡有公車站。）

Question: Which bus will the man take?

　　　（問題：那個男人將搭哪一個公車？）

(A)No. 2.（二號。）

(B)No. 22.（二十二號。）

(C)No. 21.（二十一號。）

(D)No. 12.（十二號。）

答案：(D)

IV、Listen to the passage and decide whether the following statements are True (T) or

False (F). (判斷下列句子內容是否符合你所聽到的短文內容，符合的用"T" 表示，不符合的用"F" 表示。)（6分）

Today, people spend too much time on TV. (今天，人們花太多時間在電視上。)

The average American family has the TV on for 6 hours and 40 minutes every day. (一般美國家庭每天打開電視六小時四十分鐘。)

Too much television has bad effects, especially on children. (太多電視有不良影響，特別是對兒童。)

The average child watches TV for 28 hours a week. (一般兒童一星期看二十八小時的電視。)

So one organization is trying to get people to watch less TV. (所以，某一個組織正嚐試讓人人少看電視。)

It is TV-Turnoff Network. (那就是「關電視聯播網」。)

In 2002 they got 6.5 million people to stop watching TV for a week. (在 2002 年，他們使六百五十萬人一星期不看電視。)

They say, "Turn off TV, turn on life." (他們說：「關掉電視，打開生活」。)

Some Hollywood stars also support the idea of watching less TV. (一些好萊塢明星也支持少看電視的概念。)

Tom Cruise, the famous actor only allows his children to watch 3.5 hours of TV a week. (知名演員 Tom Cruise 只讓他的孩子一星期看三個半小時的電視。)

19. The average American family has the TV on for more than 7 hours every day.
    (一般美國家庭每天開電視超過七小時。)

    答案：（F 錯）

20. Children watch too much television.
    (兒童看太多電視。)

    答案：（T 對）

21. TV-Turnoff Network is asking people not to watch TV.
    (「關電視聯播網」要求人們不看電視。)

    答案：（F 錯）

22. In 2002 TV-Turnoff Network got a lot of people to stop watching TV forever.
    (2002 年，「關電視聯播網」讓許多人從此不再看電視。)

    答案：（F 錯）

23. Some Hollywood stars think it's a good idea to watch less TV.
（有一些好萊塢明星認為少看電視是一個很好的概念。）

答案：（T 對）

24. Tom Cruise allows his children to watch TV for 3.5 hours every day.
（Tom Cruise 讓他的孩子每天看三個半小時的電視。）

答案：（F 錯）

V、Listen to the passage and complete the table.（根據你所聽到的短文內容，用適當的單詞或數字完成下面的表格。每空格限填一詞或數字。）（6分）

Welcome to Yonghua Cinema.
（歡迎來到 Yonghua 電影院。）

The new film Red Cliff will be on soon.
（新片赤壁即將上映。）

It is about the Battle of Red Cliffs from the Three Kingdoms Period.
（這是關於三國時代的赤壁之戰。）

It is directed by the famous director, John Woo.
（它是由知名導演 John Wu（吳宇森）所執導。）

The film lasts for 90 minutes.
（本片長達 90 分鐘。）

The ticket costs 65 yuan.
（票價六十五元。）

You can see the film at six thirty, seven fifteen or nine thirty in the evening.
（你可以在晚上六點三十分、七點十五分或九點三十分看到這部電影。）

How can you miss such a nice film?
（你怎麼能錯過這麼好的電影？）

It will be on at Yonghua Cinema from tomorrow to 19 August.
（它將從明天開始到八月十九日在 Yonghua 電影院上映。）

Please come to our cinema and we believe you'll love it.
（請來我們電影院，我們相信你會喜歡它的。）

Film: Red Cliff（電影：赤壁）	Price: __25__ yuan（票價：＿＿＿元）
Where: Yonghua __26__	When: Ends on __27__ Aug.
（地點：Yonghua＿＿＿）	（時間：在八月＿＿＿日結束）
How long: __28__ minutes	Director: __29__ Woo
（片長：＿＿＿分鐘）	（導演：＿＿＿ 吳）
Show time: 6.30 p.m.; __30__ p.m.; 9.30 p.m.	

（上映時間：晚上六點三十分、晚上＿＿＿、晚上九點三十分）

25. 答案：65

26. 答案：Cinema (電影院)

27. 答案：19

28. 答案：90

29. 答案：John

30. 答案：7.15

I、Listen and choose the right picture.（根據你聽到的內容,選出相應的圖片。）（6分）

1. Sammy dreams of traveling around the world with his pet dog Charlie.
    （桑密夢想著和他的寵物狗查理一起到世界各地旅行。）
    答案：(F)

2. This article is about a popular baseball player who is always kind to his fans.
    （這篇文章是關於一位受歡迎的棒球選手，他總是對他的球迷很好。）
    答案：(G)

3. The well-known actress sent his son to school and said goodbye to him.
    （這位知名的女星送她兒子去上學並和他說再見。）
    答案：(E)

4. Roy and Ray want to find a judge as they plan to have a tennis match.
    （羅伊和雷想要找個裁判，因為他們計劃打一場網球賽。）
    答案：(C)

5. Alice asks Jane about the riddle in the newspaper, but she can't work it out.
    （愛莉斯問珍關於報紙裡的謎語，但是她解不出來。）
    答案：(B)

6. Tommy asks his mother to see his report while she is cooking dinner.
    （湯米要求他母親看他的的報告，當她正在煮晚餐的時候。）
    答案：(A)

7.　M: There will be a fireworks show in the Century Park tomorrow. Would you like to go with me?

（男：明天在世紀公園會有一場煙火秀。妳想跟我去嗎？）

W: I'd love to. But I have to visit my grandma with my aunt.

（女：我很想。但是我必須和我阿姨一起去拜訪我祖母。）

M: That's all right. Say hello to your grandma for me.

（男：沒關係。幫我像妳的祖母問好。）

Q: What will the girl do tomorrow?（問題：這位女孩明天會做什麼？）

(A)Visit her aunt.（拜訪她的阿姨。）　　　(B)See her grandma.（去看她祖母。）

(C)Watch the show.（看那場秀。）　　　(D)Go to the park. （去公園。）

答案：(B)

8.　M: Jane, have you got your exam report?（男：珍，妳拿到妳的成績單了嗎？）

W: Yes, Dad. I will show it to you.（女：是的，爸。我會拿給你看。）

M: OK. You get A grades in math and physics. Congratulations!

（男：好。妳在數學和物理拿到 A。恭喜！）

W: Thanks, Dad. But I get C in English and B in Chinese. What should I do?

（女：謝謝爸。但是我在英文拿到 C 而中文拿到 B。我該怎麼辦？）

M: Don't worry. To read more is always useful.（男：別擔心。多讀書總是有用的。）

Q: Which subjects is the girl weak in?（問題：這位女孩弱在哪一科？）

(A)Math and physics.（數學和物理。）

(B)Physics and Chinese.（物理和中文。）

(C)English and math.（英文和數學。）

(D)English and Chinese.（英文和中文。）

答案：(D)

9.　M: Excuse me, is Mrs. Wang at the office?（男：請問，王太太在辦公室嗎？）

W: She has gone to London. She won't be back until next week.

（女：她去倫敦了。她直到下星期都不會回來。）

M: I see. May I meet her next Friday?

（男：我明白了。我可以下星期五和她見面嗎？）

W: You can call again next Thursday.（女：你可以下星期四再打電話來。）

Q: When will Mrs. Wang return?（問題：王太太什麼時候會回來？）

(A)Next Monday.（下星期一。）　　　(B)Next Friday.（下星期五。）

(C)Next Wednesday.（下星期三。）　　　(D)Next Thursday.（下星期四。）

答案：(D)

10.　M: How can I get to the zoo?（男：我怎樣可以到動物園？）

W: You'd better not drive there as the gate is far from the parking lot.
（女：你最好不要開車去那裡，因為大門離停車場很遠。）

M: Can I call a taxi?（男：我可以叫計程車嗎？）

W: What's the difference? The underground will go right there.
（女：那有什麼兩樣？地鐵會直達那邊。）

Q: How does the woman suggest the man go to the zoo?
（問題：這位女士建議這位男士如何去動物園？）

(A)By metro.（搭地鐵。）　　　　　　(B)By taxi.（搭計程車。）

(C)By car.（開車。）　　　　　　　(D)On foot.（走路。）

答案：(A)

11. M: Who is that woman?（男：那位女士是誰？）

W: Which woman?（女：哪位女士？）

M: The one with long hair.（男：那位有長頭髮的。）

W: She is the class teacher of Class Four and the other one with short hair is the class teacher of Class Ten. They are both 37 years old.（女：她是四班的班導師，而另一位短頭髮的是十班的班導師。她們都是三十七歲。）

Q: Which statement is not true?（問題：哪個說明是不正確的？）

(A)The woman with long hair is 37 years old.（長頭髮的女士是三十七歲。）

(B)The woman with short hair is a teacher.（短頭髮的女士是一位老師。）

(C)The class teacher of Class Ten has long hair.（十班的班導師有長頭髮。）

(D)The class teacher of Class Four is 37 years old.（四班的班導師是三十七歲。）

答案：(C)

12. M: What's this? It looks so strange.（男：這是什麼？它看起來好怪。）

W: So strange? It is worth 1 million dollars.（女：好怪嗎？它值一百萬美金。）

M: How do you know that?（男：妳怎麼知道？）

W: It is a bowl made of special stone one thousand years ago.
（女：這是一個一千年前以特殊石材製造的碗。）

M: What a pity it is that my father isn't here now. He has much interest in ancient things.（男：我父親現在不在這裡真可惜。他對古老的東西很有興趣。）

Q: Where does this dialogue take place?（問題：這段對話在哪裡發生？）

(A)In a bookstore.（在書店。）　　　　(B)At the bank.（在銀行。）

(C)In the post office.（在郵局。）　　　(D)In a museum.（在博物館。）

答案：(D)

13. M: Mary, can you tell me Mrs. Lin's cell phone number?
（男：瑪莉，妳可以告訴我林太太的行動電話號碼嗎？）

W: OK. It is 13817273749.（女：好的。是 13817273749。）

M: Thank you so much. Er, wait, why does the receiver say that the number doesn't exist?（男：

多謝妳。呃，等等，為何電話那頭說此號碼不存在？）

W: Let me check. I am so sorry that the second seven should be five.

（女：讓我檢查一下。我很抱歉，第二個七應該是五。）

Q: What is the right number of Mrs. Lin's cell phone?

（問題：林太太行動電話的正確號碼是？）

(A)13815273749.   (B)13817253749.   (C)13817273549.   (D)13817273745.

答案：(B)

14. M: Rebecca, how about your Math exam? You are always the top in our class.

（男：瑞貝卡，妳數學考得怎麼樣？妳總是我們班上的第一。）

W: Thanks. But this time I made three mistakes in Choice which cost me two points each because I didn't pay attention to the definitions in the book.（女：謝謝。但是這次我在選擇題犯了三個錯，每題讓我失去兩分，因為我沒有注意書上的定義。）

M: It's just because of your carelessness. Forget it and I think you will soon get 100 again.（男：只是因為妳的不小心。忘了吧，我想妳很快就會再次考一百分。）

W: I will work harder. Let's wait and see.（女：我會更用功。讓我們等著瞧。）

Q: What is the score of Rebecca's math exam?（問題：瑞貝卡的數學考試得幾分？）

(A)94 points.（九十四分）   (B)96 points.（九十六分）

(C)98 points.（九十八分）   (D)100 points.（一百分）

答案：(A)

15. M: What's the name of the program?（男：這節目名稱是什麼？）

W: It's called "Day Day Up".（女：它叫作「日日升」。）

M: But why do I often see lots of stars giving performances on the stage?

（男：但是為什麼我常常看到很多明星在舞台上表演？）

W: I think they also represent part of the culture and we can learn something as well.（女：我想他們也代表文化的一部分而我們也可以學點什麼。）

Q: What are they talking about?（問題：他們在談論什麼？）

(A)How to study well.（如何把書念好。）

(B)Super stars.（超級明星。）

(C)A TV program.（一個電視節目。）

(D)Daily news.（每日新聞。

答案：(C)

16. M: Where would you like to further your study?（男：妳想在哪裡繼續妳的學業？）

W: France is famous for art while in London, I can learn about economy.

（女：法國在藝術方面很有名，而在倫敦我可以學經濟方面。）

M: Last time I was told that you were interested in financial analysis.

（男：上次我聽說妳對金融分析有興趣。）

W: Yes. If I decide to learn it, I have to choose Harvard University.

（女：對。如果我決定學這個，我必須選哈佛大學。）

Q: If the girl wants to learn something related to finance, where should she go to further her study?（問題：如果這位女孩想學和金融有關的一些東西，她應該去哪裡繼續她的學業？）

(A)England.（英國）
(B)France.（法國）
(C)America.（美國）
(D)Germany.（德國）

答案：(C)

Ⅲ、Listen to the passage and tell whether the following statements are true or false.（判斷下列句子是否符合你聽到的短文內容,符合用 T 表示,不符合用 F 表示）(7分)

A young traveler was exploring the Alps. He came upon a big empty land. It was like the wasteland. It was the kind of place you hurry away from.

一位年輕的旅人正在探索阿爾卑斯山脈。他來到一大片空地上。它像是一片荒原。它是那種你會快快離開的地方。

Then, suddenly, the young traveler stopped dead to have a rest. In the middle of this big wasteland was a bent-over old man. On his back was a bag of seeds. In his hand was a four-foot-long iron pipe.

然後，忽然，這位年輕旅人停下來靜止著休息。在這一大片荒原中間有一位彎著腰的老人。在他的背上是一袋種子。在他手裡是一根四尺長的鐵管。

The old man was using the iron pipe to dig holes in the ground. Then from the bag he would take a seed and put it in the hole. Later the old man told the traveler, "I've planted 100,000 seeds. Perhaps only one tenth of them will grow." The old man's wife and son had died, and this was how he chose to spend his final years. "I want to do something useful," he said.

這位老人正在用這根鐵管往地上挖洞。然後他會從袋子裡拿出一顆種子放到洞裡。之後這位老人告訴這位旅人，「我種了十萬顆種子。或許它們當中只有十分之一會長出來。」這位老人的妻子和兒子已經死了，而這是他選擇度過餘生的方式。「我想要做些有用的事，」他說。

Twenty-five years later the now-not-as-young traveler returned to the same place. What he saw amazed him. He could not believe his own eyes. The land was covered with a beautiful forest two miles wide and five miles long. Birds were singing, animals were playing, and wild flowers perfumed the air.

二十五年後不再那麼年輕的旅人回到了同一個地方。他所看到的讓他驚奇。他無法相信他的眼睛。這塊地被兩英里寬五英里長美麗的森林覆蓋著。鳥兒在唱歌，動物在嬉戲，而野花們使空氣芳香。

The traveler stood there recalling the wilderness that once was; a beautiful forest stood there now — all because someone cared.

這位旅人站在那裡回想著曾經一度的荒廢景像；現在一片美麗的森林矗立在那

裡 — 全因為某個人關心。

17. A young traveler lost his way on the Alps.
（一位年輕的旅人在阿爾卑斯山脈迷路了。）
答案：(F 錯)

18. An old man with magic power saved the traveler's life.
（一位有魔法的老人救了這位旅人的命。）
答案：(F 錯)

19. The old man used a metal pipe to dig a hole where the seed could be put.
（這位老人用一根金屬管在要放種子的地方挖洞。）
答案：(T 對)

20. The old man lived alone and wanted to do something useful.
（這位老人獨居，想要做些有用的事。）
答案：(T 對)

21. The traveler came to the place again twenty years later.
（這位旅人二十年後再次來到這個地方。）
答案：(F 錯)

22. The wasteland disappeared and the land looked beautiful and smelt nice.
（荒原消失了，這片地看起來美麗且氣味芬芳。）
答案：(T 對)

23. The writer saw the 100,000 trees and was thankful to the old man.
（筆者看到十萬棵樹，對老人很感激。）
答案：(F 錯)

IV、Listen to the passage and fill in the blanks with proper words.（聽短文,用最恰當的詞填空,每格限填一詞）（共 7 分）

The tourist guide book has gone digital in Japan. New technology that sends data to a hand held screen is being tried in Tokyo. It can tell you where you are, the history of landmarks and buildings, and the shopping secrets of the city.

在日本觀光導遊書籍已進入數位化。可以把新資料送到一個手持螢幕的新科技已在東京試用。它可以告訴你在哪裡、地標和建築物的歷史，還有此都市的購物秘訣。

Tokyo is a busy international city. But it's also easy to feel puzzled by all the buildings, shops, neon lights and crowded streets around you.

東京是個忙碌的國際都市。但也很容易感到被你周圍所有的建築物、店鋪、霓虹燈和擁擠街道所迷惑的地方。

But now help is at hand, in the form of a small device. Like a smart phone, it can receive useful information on your exact location, where to eat and where to shop.

但是現在幫助就在手邊，以一個小裝置的型態。像個智慧型手機，它可以接收關於你精確的所在地的有用資訊，去哪裡吃、去哪裡購物。

People can walk through the city and learn about it as they go.

人們可以走路穿越此都市並在行動中了解它。

And locals can have some fun with it too.

當地人也可以從它得到一些樂趣。

One tourist said, "I think it's useful and it's faster than a normal map and it's easy to use. I think it would be better to use this tool in all of the city and not just here in the center."

一位觀光客說，「我認為它很有用而且它比普通地圖更快又易於使用。我認為在整個都市都用這個工具會比較好，而不是只在位居中心的這裡。」

The technology is being developed by the Tokyo Government.

此科技正被東京政府開發中。

"Anyone, any time, anywhere" is the project motto and that's what the system delivers.

「任何人、任何時候、在任何地方」是此企劃的座右銘，正是這個系統所給予的。

- In Japan, a new electronic __24__ book has appeared.
  （在日本，一個新的電子導遊書已出現。）

- The books tell where you are, the history of landmarks and buildings, and the shopping __25__ of the city.
  （這些書告訴你在哪裡、地標和建築物的歷史、和此都市的購物祕訣。）

- All the buildings, shops, neon lights and __26__ streets around you make you confused in Japan.
  （在日本，你周圍所有的建築物、店鋪、霓虹燈和擁擠的街道使你迷惑。）

- The electronic book looks like a smart __27__ in appearance.
  （這電子書在外觀上看起來像個智慧型手機。）

- Travelers as well as __28__ people can have some fun with the newly-produced book.
  （旅人和當地人也都可以從這個新生產的書得到一些樂趣。）

- The book is more useful and __29__ than a normal map.
  （這本書更有用且比普通地圖更快。）

- What the system __30__ is "Anyone, any time, anywhere".
  （這個系統所給予的是「任何人、任何時候、在任何地方」。）

24. 答案：guide（導遊）
25. 答案：secrets（祕訣）
26. 答案：crowded（擁擠）
27. 答案：phone（電話）
28. 答案：local（當地）
29. 答案：faster（更快）
30. 答案：delivers（給予）

Unit 14

I、Listen and choose the right picture. (根據你所聽到的內容,選出相應的圖片。) (6分)

A　　　　　　　B　　　　　　　C

D　　　　　　　E　　　　　　　F　　　　　　　G

1.　We went to Sanya to enjoy the sea view this summer holiday.
（這個暑假我們去三亞欣賞海景。）
答案：(G)

2.　When autumn comes, leaves start falling from the trees.
（當秋天來臨的時候,樹葉開始從樹上掉落。）
答案：(F)

3.　Thunder storms always happen in summer in Shanghai.
（在上海,雷雨總是在夏天發生。）
答案：(D)

4.　Look! The little boy is making a snowman happily in the park.
（看啊!那個小男孩在公園裡快樂的堆雪人呢。）
答案：(B)

5.　In spring, it's fun to fly kites in the open area.
（春天的時候,在空曠的區域放風箏很有趣。）
答案：(C)

6. The wind begins blowing hard. （風開始猛烈的吹。）

   答案：(A)

II、Listen and choose the best response to the sentence you hear. （根據你所聽到的句子, 選出最恰當的應答句。）（6分）

---

7. May I speak to Jenny? （我能找 Jenny 說話嗎？）

   (A)I'm Jenny. （我是 Jenny。）

   (B)Yes, I am. （是的，我是。）

   (C)Sorry, she isn't here. （抱歉，她不在。）

   (D)Who are you? （你是誰？）

   答案：(C)

8. How are you and your parents? （你和你的父母都好嗎？）

   (A)We are friends. （我們是朋友。）

   (B)We are fine. Thanks. （我們很好，謝謝。）

   (C)We have been to Japan. （我們去了日本。）

   (D)We will stay at home. （我們會待在家。）

   答案：(B)

9. What time will you come back? （你什麼時候回來？）

   (A)After three days. （三天之後。）   (B)At midnight. （午夜。）

   (C)Three days later. （晚三天。）   (D)Since three days. （自三天前。）

   答案：(B)

10. You look upset. Is anything wrong? （你看起來很沮喪。有甚麼問題嗎？）

    (A)I've lost my key rings. （我掉了我的鑰匙。）

    (B)I'm 15 years old. （我十五歲。）

    (C)I will buy a new shirt. （我要買一件新襯衫。）

    (D)I am right. （我是對的。）

    答案：(A)

11. How much is the ticket? （票價多少？）

    (A)To Beijing. （到北京。）

    (B)100 yuan. （一百元。）

    (C)At five in the afternoon. （在下午五點。）

    (D)It's for sale. （拍賣中。）

    答案：(B)

12. Robin, this is my mother. Mum, this is my friend, Robin.
    （Robin, 這位是我母親。媽，這是我的朋友 Robin。）

(A)Bye bye. （再見。）

(B)Hello. Nice to meet you. （哈囉，很高興認識你。）

(C)What's your name? （你的大名是？）

(D)Who's your friend? （你的朋友是誰？）

答案：(B)

Ⅲ、Listen to the dialogue and choose the best answer to the question you hear. （根據你所聽到的對話和問題,選出最恰當的答案。）(6分)

13. W: Has the train left? （W: 火車離開了嗎？）

M: No, it is leaving in ten minutes. And it's three forty now.

（M: 還沒，它十分鐘後離開。現在是三點四十分。）

Q: When is the train leaving? （Q: 火車何時離開？）

(A)3:30. （三點三十分。）　　　　　　(B)3:40. （三點四十分。）

(C)3:50. （三點五十分。）　　　　　　(D)4:00. （四點。）

答案：(C)

14. W: What does winter make you think of? （W: 冬天讓你想起甚麼？）

M: Winter makes me think of snow. What about you?

（M: 冬天讓我想起下雪。妳呢？）

W: Winter makes me think of skating. （W: 冬天讓我想起滑雪。）

Q: What does winter make the girl think of? （Q: 冬天讓女孩想起甚麼？）

(A)Snow. （下雪。）　　　　　　　　　(B)Skating. （滑雪。）

(C)Coldness. （寒冷。）　　　　　　　(D)Warm clothes. （溫暖的衣服。）

答案：(B)

15. M: What can I do for you? （M: 我能為妳效勞嗎？）

W: I'd like to buy three tickets. How much does one ticket cost?

（W: 我要買三張票。一張票多少錢？）

M: Forty yuan for an adult. Twenty yuan for a child.

（M: 成人票一張四十元。兒童票一張二十元。）

W: I need a ticket for an adult and two tickets for children.

（W: 我要一張成人票，兩張兒童票。）

Q: How much is the woman going to pay for the tickets altogether?

（Q: 那個女人一共要花多少錢買票？）

(A)80 yuan. （八十元。）　　　　　　(B)100 yuan. （一百元。）

(C)60 yuan. （六十元。）　　　　　　(D)120 yuan. （一百二十元。）

答案：(A)

16. M: Can I take these books home, please? （M: 我可以把這幾本書帶回家嗎？）

W: Yes, here you are. You can keep them for two weeks.

（W: 好的。給你。你可以保留兩個星期。）

Q: Who is the man talking to?（Q: 那個男人在對誰說話？）

(A)A shop assistant.（店員。）   (B)A book seller.（書商。）

(C)A librarian.（圖書管理員。）   (D)A secretary.（秘書。）

答案：(C)

17.   W: What's the weather like today, John?（W: John，今天天氣怎麼樣？）

M: It's cloudy and late afternoon it will rain. But the weather report says it's going to be a fine day tomorrow.

（M: 陰天，下午就會下雨了。但是氣象報告說明天天氣不錯。）

W: Really? What about going for a picnic tomorrow?

（W: 真的嗎？明天去野餐怎麼樣？）

M: That's a great idea.（M: 這真是個好主意。）

Q: What will the weather be like tomorrow?（Q: 明天天氣如何？）

(A)Rainy.（有雨。）   (B)Stormy.（暴風雨。）

(C)Foggy.（有霧。）   (D)Sunny.（晴朗。）

答案：(D)

18.   W: Dad, listen! There is big noise outside. What happens?

（W: 爸，你聽！外面有好大的噪音。發生甚麼事了？）

M: Oh! Some children are setting off firecrackers.（M: 喔！有些孩子在放鞭炮。）

W: Why do they do so?（W: 他們為什麼要這麼做？）

M: In China, it's fun for children to set off firecrackers, visit relatives and receive red packets during the Spring Festival.

（M: 在中國的春節期間，放鞭炮、拜訪親戚、拿紅包，對孩子們來說很有趣。）

Q: What don't children do during the Spring Festival?

（Q: 春節期間孩子們不做甚麼？）

(A)To eat mooncakes.（吃月餅。）   (B)To set off firecrackers.（放鞭炮。）

(C)To receive red packets.（拿紅包。）   (D)To visit relatives.（拜訪親戚。）

答案：(A)

Ⅳ、Listen to the dialogue and decide whether the following statements are True (T) or False (F).（判斷下列句子內容是否符合你所聽到的對話內容,符合的用"T"表示,不符合的用"F"表示。）（6分）

Plants 植物

We can see many plants around us every day. There are over 300,000 species of plants in the world. They play an important part in our life. Now let's see the importance of plants.

我們每天都可以在周遭看到許多植物。世界上有超過三十萬種植物。它們在我們的生活中扮演重要的角色。現在讓我們來看看植物的重要性。

Plants bring natural beauty to us. Many people like decorating their rooms with flowers or other plants. The plants in the room can make people feel comfortable and relaxed.

植物為我們帶來自然美景。許多人喜歡利用花朵或其他植物來裝飾他們的房間。房間裡的植物可以讓人們感到舒適與放鬆。

Of course, plants can do more things for people. They help people clean the air we breathe and they are just like little oxygen factories. They also help hold the soil and stop soil and water from moving away.

當然,植物可以為人們做更多事。植物有助於清潔我們呼吸的空氣,它們就像小型的氧氣工廠。它們也能抓住土壤,不讓土壤與水分流失。

Both people and animals can get food from plants. People and animals can't live without plants. Plants are useful. Workers can make furniture out of wood, clothes out of cotton, and so on. Some plants can also be used as medicine.

人和動物可以從植物中獲得食物。沒有了植物,人和動物將無法生存。植物很有用。工人可以做木製家具、棉製衣服...等等。有些植物還可以做成藥物。

Plants are really important and we should protect them and make good use of them.
植物真的很重要,我們應該要保護它們並且好好的利用它們。

19. There are more than thirty million kinds of plants in the world.
（世界上有超過三千萬種植物。）
答案：(F 錯)

20. People like decorating rooms with flowers and other plants.
（人們喜歡用花和其他植物來裝飾房間。）
答案：(T 對)

21. People and animals only get food from plants.（人和動物只從植物來獲得食物。）
答案：(F 錯)

22. Unlike animals, people can't live without plants.
（人不像動物,沒有了植物就無法生存。）
答案：(F 錯)

23. People can make clothes out of cotton.（人們可以做出棉製的衣服。）
答案：(T 對)

24. All medicines are made from plants.（所有的藥物都是從植物製造的。）
答案：(F 錯)

Almost everybody likes to play. All over the world, men and women, boys and girls enjoy sports. Sports help to keep people healthy and let them live happily.

幾乎每一個人都喜歡遊玩。全世界的男人、女人、男孩、女孩都喜歡運動。運動有助於人們維持健康,活得快樂。

Sports change with the seasons. People play different games in winter and summer. Sailing is fun in warm weather, while skating is good in winter.

運動隨著季節而改變。人們在冬天和夏天玩不一樣的運動遊戲。在溫暖的天氣划船很有趣,然而在冬天滑雪就很棒。

People from different areas may not be able to understand each other, but after a game on the sports field, they often become good friends. Sports help to train a person's character. One learns to fight hard, to win without pride and to lose with grace.

不同地區的人們不一定彼此了解,但是在運動場上的一場比賽之後,他們常常會變成好朋友。運動有助於訓練一個人的個性,學習奮力拼博,勝不驕,敗不餒。

25. Sports help to keep people healthy and make them live <u>happily</u>.
運動有助於人們維持健康,活得<u>快樂</u>。

26. Sports change with the <u>seasons</u>.
運動隨著<u>季節</u>而改變。

27. Sailing is <u>fun</u> in warm weather.
在溫暖的天氣划船很<u>有趣</u>。

28. <u>Skating</u> is good in winter.
在冬天<u>滑雪</u>很棒。

29. People from different <u>areas</u> may not be able to understand each other, but after a game on the sports field, they often become good friends.
不同<u>地區</u>的人們不一定彼此了解,但是在運動場上的一場比賽之後,他們常常會變成好朋友。

30. One learns to fight hard, to win without pride and to <u>lose</u> with grace.
一個人學習奮力拼博,勝不驕和<u>敗</u>不餒。

Unit 15

I、Listen and choose the right picture.

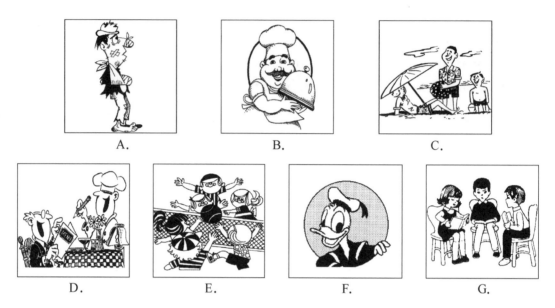

A.	B.	C.

| D. | E. | F. | G. |

1. Can't you see the ball's coming? Hey! Stop them, Peter!
    (你看不到球正飛過來嗎？嘿！阻止他們，彼得！)
    答案：(E)

2. Donald Duck is one of the most popular characters in Walt Disney's cartoons.
    (唐老鴨是華德迪士尼的卡通中最受歡迎的角色之一。)
    答案：(F)

3. Don't lie under the umbrella! Put on your swimming suit and let's go to the sea.
    (不要躺在傘下！穿上妳的泳裝一起到海裡去吧。)
    答案：(C)

4. Sir, may I have your order now? (先生，我現在可以為您點餐了嗎？)
    答案：(D)

5. What's the matter with you, Billy? Was there an accident just now?
    (你是怎麼了，比利？剛才是不是發生了一場意外？)
    答案：(A)

6. Do you know this word, Ben and Mary? You can look it up in your book!
    (班和瑪莉，你們認識這個字嗎？你們可以在你們的書裡查查它。)
    答案：(G)

7. W: What time shall we start for Shanghai International Financial Centre?
    (女：我們應該幾點出發去上海國際金融中心？)

    M: How about a quarter to eight? (男：七點四十五分如何？)

    W: No, let's make it thirty-five minutes later because it is not very far from here.
    (女：不，讓我們晚個三十五分鐘因為它距離這邊不很遠。)

    Question: When will they start for Shanghai International Financial Centre?
    (問題：他們幾點會出發去上海國際金融中心？)

    (A)7.45.   (B)8.20.   (C)8.15.   (D)8.25.
    答案：(B)

8. M: Hello, may I speak to May? (男：哈囉，我可以和玫講話嗎？)

    W: Sorry. She has gone to the library. Can I take a message for her?
    (女：抱歉。她去圖書館了。我可以幫您留話給她嗎？)

    M: Thank you. This is Jack. Please tell her that I have changed my phone number. It used to be
    56940213. But now it is 56639304. (男：謝謝。我是傑克。請告訴她我更改了我的電話
    號碼。本來是 56940213。但現在是 56639304。)

    Question: What is Jack's telephone number now? (問題：傑克現在的電話號碼是？)

    (A)56940213.   (B)56942310.   (C)56639304.   (D)56693304.
    答案：(C)

9. W: Good evening, sir. What can I do for you? (女：晚安，先生。我能為您做什麼？)

    M: Good evening. My name is Steven. I have booked a room here.
    (男：晚安。我名叫史蒂芬。我在這裡預定了一個房間。)

    W: Let me see. Oh, yes. Your room is Room 5018. Your ID card, please!
    (女：讓我看看。喔，對。您的房間是 5018 號房。請借我您的身分證！)

    Question: Where are they talking now? (問題：他們現在在哪裡對話？)

    (A)At the reception desk.(在接待櫃台)

    (B)In Room 5018. (在 5018 房內)

    (C)In a restaurant. (在餐廳)

    (D)In a bookshop. (在書店)

    答案：(A)

10. M: My brother will get to Shanghai in two hours. How shall we go to the airport?
    (男：我兄弟將在兩小時內到上海。我們該怎麼去機場？)

    W: Shall we go there by underground or by bus? (女：我們應該搭地鐵或搭巴士去？)

    M: Neither. It will take us a lot of time. I think we'd better take a taxi instead of the
    underground or a bus. (男：都不好。那將會花很多時間。我想我們最好搭計程車而非地
    鐵或巴士。)

    W: OK. (女：好。)

Question: How will they get to the airport? (問題：他們將如何去機場？)

(A)By train.(搭火車)   (B)By bus. (搭巴士)

(C)By underground. (搭地鐵)   (D)By taxi. (搭計程車)

答案：(D)

11. M: Would you like to go to the cinema with me this afternoon?

     (男：妳今天下午想跟我去看電影嗎？)

  W: I'd love to, but my mother will come back from Canada this afternoon, so I have to meet her at the airport and we will have a big meal tonight.

    (女：我很想去，但是我母親今天下午將從加拿大回來，所以我必須去機場接她然後我們今晚將吃頓大餐。)

  M: May I go with you? I haven't seen your mother for a long time.

    (男：我可以跟妳一起去嗎？我很久沒見到妳母親了。)

  W: That's great. (女：那太好了。)

  Question: What will the man do this afternoon? (問題：這位男士今天下午將做什麼？)

(A)Go to the cinema. (去看電影)   (B)Have a big meal. (吃大餐)

(C)Stay at home. (待在家)   (D)Go to the airport. (去機場)

答案：(D)

12. W: May I take your order now? (女：我現在可以為您點餐了嗎？)

  M: Yes. I think we are ready to order. (男：好的。我想我們準備好點餐了。)

  W: What would you like? (女：您想吃什麼？)

  Question: Where does this conversation probably take place?

  (問題：這段對話可能是在哪裡發生？)

(A)At a restaurant. (在餐廳。)   (B)In a hotel. (在旅館)

(C)In a supermarket. (在超市)   (D)At the cinema. (在電影院)

答案：(A)

13. W: Well, Mr White, I've completed my examination and there is nothing serious with your baby.

    (女：嗯，懷特先生，我已完成了我的檢查而您的嬰兒沒有什麼嚴重問題。)

  M: Don't you think she should take an X-ray? (男：妳不認為她應該照個X光嗎？)

  Question: What job does the woman do? (問題：這位女士是做什麼職業的？)

(A)A dentist. (牙醫)   (B)A doctor. (醫師。)   (C)A teacher. (老師)   (D)A trainer. (訓練員)

答案：(B)

14. W: You speak English very fluently. (女：你英語說得很流利。)

  M: Thank you. (男：謝謝。)

  W: How long have you learned English?(女：你學英文多久了？)

  M: I've learned English since twelve years ago. My mother began to teach me when I was four years old. (男：我從十二年前開始學英文。我母親在我四歲的時候開始教我。)

  Question: How old is the man? (問題：這位男士幾歲？)

(A)12 years old.   (B)14 years old.   (C)15 years old.   (D)16 years old.

答案：(D)

15. W: My dog doesn't seem to be as friendly as yours. (女：我的狗似乎不像你的那麼友善。)

M: I don't think so. Yours is much friendlier than mine.

（男：我不這樣認為。妳的比我的友善多了。）

Question: What does the woman think of the man's dog?

(問題：這位女士認為這位男士的狗如何？)

(A)Friendlier. (比較友善。)

(B)Not friendly. (不友善)

(C)Not as friendly as hers. (不像她的狗那麼友善)

(D)As friendly as hers. (跟她的狗一樣友善)

答案：(A)

16. W: Why did your father hurry off yesterday? (女：為何你的父親昨天匆忙離開？)

M: He was afraid that he would miss the plane. (男：他恐怕他會錯過班機。)

Question: Why did the boy's father hurry off? (問題：為何這位男孩的父親匆忙離開？)

(A)He got up late this morning. (他今天晚起床。)

(B)He hurried off to catch a plane. (他匆忙離開去趕飛機。)

(C)He was afraid that he would be late for the train. (他怕趕不上火車。)

(D)He hurried off to catch a train. (他匆忙去趕火車。)

答案：(B)

Ⅲ、Listen to the passage and decide whether the following statements are True (T) or False (F).

Good afternoon, and welcome to England. We hope that your visit will be a pleasant one. Today, I would like to draw your attention to a few of our laws.

午安，歡迎到英國。我希望你們的旅程將是愉快的。今天，我想請大家注意我們的幾條法令。

The first one is about drinking. Now, you may not buy wine in this country if you are under 18 years old. Neither may your friends. They may not buy it for you.

第一條是關於飲酒。現在，在這個國家你如果低於十八歲就不能購買酒。你的朋友們也不行。他們不能幫你買。

Secondly, noise. Enjoy yourself as you like, but please don't make unnecessary noise, especially at night. We ask you to show your friendliness to others who may wish to be quiet.

第二，噪音。你可以隨意享受，但是請不要製造不必要的噪音，特別是在晚上。我們要求你對那些可能希望你安靜的其他人表示出你的友善。

Thirdly, crossing the road. Be careful. The traffic moves on the left side of the road in this country. Use the pedestrian crossing and take great care when crossing the road.

第三，過馬路。要小心。在這個國家交通靠馬路的左邊前進。使用人行穿越道並且在過馬路時加緊小心。

My next point is about litter. It is against the law to drop litter in the street. When you have something to throw away, please put it in your pocket and take it home, or put it in a litter bin. Finally it is also against the law to buy cigarettes if you are under 16 years of age.

我的下一個重點是關於垃圾。在街道上丟垃圾是違反法律的。當你有些東西要丟棄，請將它放在你的口袋並帶回家，或將它放到垃圾桶。最後如果你的年齡低於十六歲購買香菸也是違法的。

I'd like to finish by saying that if you need any sort of help or assistance, you should get in touch with your local police station. They will be very pleased to help you.

我想以此作為結語：如果你需要任何方面的幫忙或協助，你應該連絡你當地的警察局。他們會很樂意幫助你。

Now, are there any questions?

現在，有任何問題嗎？

17. According to the passage, the listeners might be the people in the city.
(根據此短文，聽眾們可能是本市的人們。)
答案：(F 錯)

18. In this country, if you are under 18 years of age, you may not buy wine, but your friend can buy it for you.
(在這個國家，如果你年齡低於十八歲，你不能買酒，但是你的朋友們可以幫你買。)
答案：(F 錯)

19. The speaker told the listeners not to make unnecessary noise at night. But they can in the day time. (講者告訴聽眾們晚上不要製造不必要的噪音。但是他們在白天可以。)
答案：(F 錯)

20. It's important for the listeners to cross the streets by using the pedestrian crossings in England.
(在英國過馬路時使用人行穿越道對聽眾們來說是很重要的。)
答案：(T 對)

21. You may buy cigarettes if you are above 16 years of age.
(如果你年齡超過十六歲你就可以購買香菸。)
答案：(T 對)

22. It is against the law to put the litter in your pocket and take it home.
(把垃圾放在你的口袋並且帶回家是違反法律的。)
答案：(F 錯)

23. A policeman probably makes the speech. (或許是一位警察在演講。)
答案：(T 對)

IV、Listen to the dialogue and fill in the blanks.

Simon: Welcome to the programme. Today, Auntie Wang is here with us to answer your questions. Your first question is about blind people. Auntie Wang, can blind people hear better than other people?

賽門：歡迎加入課程。今天，王阿姨來到我們當中來回答你們的問題。你們的第一個問題是關於盲人。王阿姨，盲人比其他人聽得更清楚嗎？

Wang: No. Good listening skills are very useful for blind people, but they don't hear better than other people. They just use their hearing more than people with sight.

王：不。好的聆聽技巧對盲人來說很有用，但他們並不比其他人聽得更清楚。他們只是比看得到的人更常運用他們的聽覺。

Simon: What about deaf people? Can deaf people do things more easily than blind people?

賽門：聽障人士如何？聽障人士比盲人做起事情來要容易嗎？

Wang: Yes. Deaf people can do most things without any help, while blind people often need help when they go to new places or do new things.

王：是的。聽障人士可在不用幫忙之下做大部分事情，然而當去到新的場所或做新的事情時盲人經常需要幫助。

Simon: Many listeners asked, "Why can't many deaf people speak?" Can you explain that, Auntie Wang?

賽門：很多聽眾問到，「為何很多聽障人士不能講話？」您可以解釋一下嗎，王阿姨？

Wang: Yes, of course. The reason is quite simple. When people learn to speak, they listen first, and then speak. Some deaf people are not able to speak because they never get the chance to hear the language.

王：好，當然。原因頗簡單。當人們學習講話，他們先聽，然後講話。有些聽障人士無法講話因為他們從來沒有機會聽到這個語言。

Simon: How do they communicate then?

賽門：那麼他們如何溝通呢？

Wang: They usually use sign language to "talk".

王：他們通常使用手語來「講話」。

Simon: Interesting. Well, now all of our listeners know more about blind and deaf people. Auntie Wang, thank you for coming today.

賽門：真有趣。好，現在我們全體聽眾對盲人和聽障人士有更多了解了。王阿姨，謝謝您今天過來。

Wang: It was a pleasure.

王：樂意之至。

For blind people(關於盲人)

- good __24__ skills are useful for them (好的聆聽技巧對他們來說很有用)
- they __25__ hear better than other people (他們不比其他人聽得更清楚)
- they use their hearing __26__ than people with __27__
  (他們比看得到的人更常用他們的聽覺)

For deaf people(關於聽障人士)
- they do things more __28__ than blind people (他們比盲人做事情更容易)
- they never get the __29__ to hear the language (他們從來沒有機會聽到這個語言)
- they use __30__ language to communicate (他們使用手語來溝通)

24. 答案：listening
25. 答案：don't
26. 答案：more
27. 答案：sight
28. 答案：easily
29. 答案：chance
30. 答案：sign

全新國中會考英語聽力精選【下】

出版者：夏朵文理補習班

出版發行：禾耘圖書文化有限公司

地址：新北市新店區安祥路109巷15號

電話：02-29422385　傳真：02-29426087

劃撥帳號：50231111禾耘圖書文化有限公司

總經銷：紅螞蟻圖書有限公司

地址：台北市114內湖區舊宗路2段121巷28號4樓

網站：www.e-redant.com

電話：02-27953656　傳真：02-27954100

劃撥帳號：16046211紅螞蟻圖書有限公司

ISBN：978-986-94976-2-6　（下冊：平裝)

出版日期:106年6月

本書由華東師範大學出版社有限公司授權

夏朵文理補習班出版發行

定價400元